Long Gone

Part 1 – The Ending

Nick S. Bateman

Anti-Social Media Presents:

Long Gone Tomorrow
Part 1 – The Ending
Sometimes bad things happen to good people, and then those good people have to do bad things just to survive.
When a man's family dies due to a viral outbreak that was downplayed and taken far too lightly by both the government and the citizens at large, he decides to give everyone a serious wake-up call and unleashes a far more deadly virus himself. As the virus spreads and the world falls apart the lines between right or wrong and good or evil become very gray as a handful of survivors attempt to find some sort of safety in a world that is burning down around them.
Follow the stories of five survivors as they experience the fall of mankind and the brutality of a world without society and sorely lacking in humanity.

Part 1: Thinning the Herd

1.

"Did you know," Thomas said to the memory of his dead wife as he removed the screws from the air conditioning vent, "that one sick person at an international airport can cause a worldwide pandemic? All those people in there rubbing against each other, coughing, and breathing on each other, it's like a giant petri dish!"

He finally released the last screw from the grate covering the main inlet shaft into the airport's ventilation system and then threw the screwdriver into the toolbox at his feet.

"There we go," he said. "We're on the home stretch Sherry-berry!"

He pulled a canister out of the toolbox and held it up where he could examine it. The canister had been modified with a motorized mechanical release valve which was attached to a timer. He admired his work for a moment, work that had taken over a year and a half to complete, and then set the timer for 30 minutes and placed the canister into the duct in front of him. He replaced the grate on the ventilation system so the dispersant wouldn't drift out instead of into the airport as he wanted.

"There," he said calmly. "All done my love. They'll take this seriously... if any of them live through it."

He stepped over the corpse of the maintenance worker at his feet who had made the mistake of questioning who he was and why he was in the HVAC room of the airport. Thomas had swiftly shoved his Ka-Bar Gunny knife threw the man's chin and directly into his brain killing him instantly just as he'd been taught. The man didn't even have a chance to defend himself and had been dead before he even knew he'd been stabbed. Two years ago, Thomas would have never murdered an innocent civilian, but the last two years had made him realize that almost none of these people are innocent... also, if this worked out most of them would be dead in a few weeks anyway.

Thomas adjusted the hat he was wearing so it shaded his face well, then walked out the door of the HVAC room that opened onto the maintenance hall of the airport. He only had 25 minutes left to get out of this place before he, like the rest of these selfish and vacuous morons, would be infected with the most aggressive and deadly virus Thomas could manage to whip up with the help of a CRISPR kit he'd ordered online. He was no scientist and had no working knowledge of genetics or virology, and he thought he would have trouble doing what he wanted to do, but once he got the kit and did a bit of Googling, he had been able to do exactly what he'd wanted rather quickly and easily.

In just 23 minutes a mutated form of Rabies, piggybacking on a mutated strain of SARS, would infect the thousands of people in this airport. Those people would then travel across the globe and transmit the infection to thousands more until the thousands grew to millions and even trillions. Thomas figured that a scientist somewhere would figure out a vaccine, but not before millions of people had contracted this shit and died just as horribly as his wife and children had. He'd had to watch them choke to death, one after another, and then he'd had to watch people protest in the streets over having to wear a fucking mask when they were in public so they wouldn't potentially infect others with the same disease that killed his whole family. The president had inferred that Thomas' family had been an acceptable loss and that his administration had done all they could to protect the citizens from the disease, but they all knew that was bullshit. But apparently, they didn't all know that was bullshit because in November of 2020, just a month after Thomas had buried his youngest daughter Kira and the last of his family to die, enough people actually voted for that lying conman to have a second term. That had been the final straw for Thomas.

2.

Thomas climbed behind the wheel of his car in the short-term parking section of the Reagan National Airport and looked at his watch. He'd gotten out with 5 minutes to spare, but that was cutting it closer than he liked. He wanted to see this play out so he couldn't afford to get infected himself. Still, he sat looking at his watch, a present his wife had gotten him for their 12th wedding anniversary and let those last 5 minutes pass before looking up again at the airport. It wasn't like a bomb or mass shooting where the effect is immediate and you get that sense of instant gratification, but a feeling of calm satisfaction fell over Thomas. He closed his eyes for a moment and remembered his wife and daughters, then started the car and began the long drive back to Tennessee.

3.

The first report of the outbreak came 1 week later but was reported as a SARS outbreak that was resistant to treatment. The reports were bad, saying that over 15,000 known cases had been documented and that they were in the process of trying to trace back to the origin of the outbreak. Within 24 hours that number had doubled and over 20 other countries had reported infections, but there were still no reports of Rabies.

Then, after 3 days of watching nothing but the news and the number of reported cases triple and quadruple, Thomas saw a report that one of the first patients had started showing signs of recovery.

Thomas thought he must have messed up somehow and had only managed to give a lot of folks a bad case of SARS. Over the course of the day reports kept coming in that the first patients were getting better. With every story Thomas became more depressed and angrier. He finally got sick of seeing the news and decided he'd just have a few drinks and sit on the porch. He went to the fridge and found he'd drank all the beers he'd had in there over the last few days. "Fuck," he said to no one and grabbed his keys off the rack beside the back door.

He drove down to Applebee's to have some drinks and just stare at whatever sports event they had showing. Halfway through his 4th beer the television Thomas had been staring a hole into flashed the words "Breaking News!" across the screen. The sound was turned down, but Thomas read at the bottom of the screen "Histeria in D.C. hospital as outbreak patients turn violent and attack staff...".

"Hey," Thomas said to the bartender. "Can you turn that up please? It looks important."

The bartender glanced up at the screen and saw the banner at the bottom. "Oh shit." He said and grabbed the remote under the bar to turn the television's volume up.

"...our own Sam Collins on the scene. Sam," the reporter on the screen said as the volume came up mid-sentence.

"As you can see Tim, police have barricaded off the hospital and aren't allowing anyone any closer than this," the live reporter Sam said. "But reports are that several of the outbreak patients who had seemed to be recovering became extremely violent and started attacking the nurses and even other patients."

"Do you have any information on how many staff or other patients have been injured," Tim in the studio asked?

"No Tim," Sam replied. "As of now the police have not released any... Hold on Tim, there seems to be movement at the front doors."

The camera panned away from Sam over to the front doors of the hospital and zoomed in. A young woman in a hospital gown was slowly walking out the doors pushing them with her whole body rather than her hands. The camera panned over to a line of police with their guns drawn and all pointed at the doors and now the young woman emerging from the doors. The camera shot back over to the woman who was now in front of the doors and what sounded like a growl could be heard through the television. Thomas wasn't sure if that sound was coming from the woman or some sort of interference through the microphone of the news station.

One of the cops stepped towards the woman and lowered his gun.

"Ma'am," the officer said. "Are you hurt ma'am?"

The cop kept moving forward and the woman looked up. The camera zoomed in on the woman's face and Thomas could see her eyes were red like every blood vessel in them had burst. The woman opened her mouth and what came out was a mixture of a scream and a guttural growl. She lunged at the officer and began attacking him furiously. She let out another of those god-awful screams and then sunk her teeth into the cop's neck and then pulled back in a violent flash causing the officer's jugular vein to spray blood all over the sidewalk they were on. The other cops opened fire on the woman and bullets ripped through her body spraying even more blood and her brains onto the sidewalk. The screen went black for a moment and then a message came up proclaiming that the channel was having technical issues and would return shortly.

This was all aired live on national television.

A waitress had screamed softly when the woman attacked the cop but neither Thomas nor the bartender had paid any attention to her. Now that the television had gone quiet Thomas could hear her crying along with some of the other patrons who had seen the event on the many televisions mounted on the walls of the Applebee's. Along with the crying were murmurs of, "Oh my God," and, "What happened," from those who had not seen. Thomas surveyed them all and saw fear and confusion on all their faces.

The bartender turned to Thomas and said, "Was that a terrorist attack or something?"

The news came back on sparing Thomas from answering that question.

Tim was back on the air and visibly shaken. "We apologize for that horrible scene of violence viewers," Tim said. "The officer who was attacked has been rushed to Medstar Georgetown listed in critical condition. Medstar Washington remains on lockdown and additional officers have been called in to assist in keeping the hospital under quarantine. Uhm... I'm being told that Sam has news right now from the Chief of Police. Sam."

"Thanks Tim," Sam said as the screen cut to the hospital. "I'm here with police chief Josh Fenriss at Medstar Washington Hospital where it seems some of the patients have become extremely violent. Chief Fenriss, do you know exactly how many of the patients have attacked people inside?"

"We uhhh, are not commenting on that at this time," Chief Fenriss said. "But I can say that S.W.A.T. is on their way and we have everything under control."

"Have people been taken hostage sir," Sam asked?

"Again, we are not commenting on that at this time," the chief responded, "but I assure you that we are more than capable of dealing with this."

Right as the chief was finishing his sentence his phone rang. He looked down at the number on the screen and said, "I have to go. We'll let you know more as we can."

"Chief Fenriss," Sam called after him, but the chief was already talking into his phone as he walked away.

Thomas had seen enough and didn't feel much like drinking any more. He threw $30 on the bar beside his empty beer bottle and did not wait for change. Only the waitress who had screamed earlier glanced at him as he left, so she was the only one who saw the smile on his face.

4.

Thomas sat transfixed in front of his television for the next 6 straight hours as reports of attacks came in from across the globe. It seemed that the infected would show signs of improvement after several days of being sick from the SARS and then become extremely violent. There was, in all that time of watching the news, no mention of Rabies at all which Thomas found extremely odd. They had to have tested some of the infected by now after the got violent and were killed, so why no mention of Rabies?

At hour seven the news was interrupted by a presidential broadcast in which the president ordered a state of emergency and national 6pm curfew. He also made no mention of Rabies, or the attacks, or how fast this thing was spreading. No mention of the CDC, or the WHO, and no mention of containment or treatment. From what anyone would gather from the 8 minutes he spent on screen, the only reason for a state of emergency was that a few riots had broken out in a few cities... which was the understatement of the year if ever there was one!

The news came back on, but Thomas wasn't interested in the mainstream media anymore, so he turned the television down some and opened his laptop. On social media there were posts about "Zombie attacks" all over the planet and riots breaking out in city after city. Religious leaders were saying it was the end times and judgement from God. Thomas knew it was neither of those things, so he scrolled past most of them and then saw what the news wasn't showing. It was another attack, and much more recent.

Someone had captured an attack by one of the infected on their cellphone and the video scared the crap out of Thomas because it was not what he had planned at all. A young man came running at another older guy trying to load stuff into his care. The younger man, whose eyes showed that fully bloodshot mark of infection, tackled the older man beside his car and began clawing at him and striking him repeatedly in the head. Then, without any warning, the infected man who had his face just a foot over the older man's face, projectile vomited a blackish substance directly on the older man's face. The older man tried to scream out and his mouth was filled with the substance which Thomas assumed was probably a mixture of blood and bile. The older man jerked violently and managed to throw his attacker off him. Then 3 shots rang out in the video and the infected attacker fell dead beside the older man. The older man was now on his knees convulsing and throwing up in his yard beside his car. A minute later a cop came into the picture and asked the older man if he was okay. The older man said nothing and continued to convulse on his knees. The cop approached the older man to try and help him, but when the cop reached the man and reached down to try to help the man to his feet, the man screamed out in a sound that reminded Thomas of the sound the woman had made before attacking the cop earlier on the news. The cop moved his hand away from the man and took a step back from him.

The older man got to his feet and turned towards the cop. His eyes had no white in them anymore and instead had gone completely bloodshot. He issued another of those eerily guttural screams and then lunged at the officer before the man had any chance to react, knocking the gun from the officer's hand as he tackled him and immediately biting off the officer's face piece by piece. Another far more human scream could be heard, probably from the person filming the incident, and then the phone fell from their hands and the video ended.

Thomas closed his laptop and sat in relative silence with the television at a low whisper for a long time. He had planned on this thing spreading quickly and being hard to contain, but this was something different entirely. Had he managed to somehow mutate the Rabies so much that its incubation period had gone from days to mere minutes? He hadn't tried to do that and couldn't see how he would have managed to do so. But he wasn't a scientist for fuck's sake, and for all he knew he'd created a virus that couldn't be stopped and spread so fast that the whole human race would be dead in less than 3 months!

This was not to plan. It was bad, and even if Thomas turned himself in and told them exactly what he'd done, he doubted anyone could stop it at this point. He stood up and began to pace an oval in his living room in front of the coffee table. He had paced for several minutes, running circles in his mind as well as his floor, when he noticed the television screen was now showing the emergency broadcast warning. He grabbed the remote and changed the channel but got the same message on the screen. He turned the volume up and heard the television say "stay indoors. This is the emergency broadcast system. This is not a test. Please be advised. A state of emergency has been declared in your area. You have been urged to stay in your home and lock your doors and windows. Do not allow anyone into your home. Police and emergency services may be unavailable due to high demand. Again, you are urged to stay indoors."

Thomas flipped the station again and was greeted by the same message and same ominous screen of noninformation. He lowered the volume again and went to the door of his apartment that faced onto 54th Avenue in Downtown Nashville and pulled a curtain aside. It looked like a normal Wednesday evening for the most part, but there wasn't much traffic. There wasn't any traffic actually and this was normally a well-used street. Because of that however, the house was well insulated, so Thomas never really heard the traffic. But he saw it all the time and got stuck in it even more.

So where was everyone?

Then he saw the headlights of his neighbor's car come on and heard the tires squeal as he rushed away. As he followed the taillights turning onto the cross street, he heard a distant scream. A few moments later there was another scream much closer. He peered out the window of his front door in the direction of the screams and could see a woman less than a block up running down the street in the same direction his neighbor had driven.

Thomas opened his door and called out to the woman, "Do you need help miss?"

The woman jerked her head in Thomas' direction and yelled out, "Oh thank God! My husband was attacked by some lunatic who kept banging on our door! He's hurt very badly and when I called 9-1-1, I got a recording."

"Where is the man who attacked your husband now," Thomas asked?

"Bobby shot him. I think he's dead," she answered.

"Stay right there," Thomas said. "Let me grab something and we'll go help your husband."

Thomas stepped back inside the door and grabbed the Beretta M9 off his coffee table and ran back out the door. As he ran down the stairs to the woman, he saw another figure running down the street towards them. Then the running figure screamed out and all the hairs on Thomas' body stood on end. It was that guttural growl of a scream he'd heard before and it stopped Thomas dead in his tracks.

The woman had turned in the direction of the scream and then Thomas heard her call out to the running figure, "Bobby? Is that you? Are you okay?"

She began walking towards the running figure and Thomas yelled to her, "Don't! Stay away from him!"

The lady turned to face Thomas and said, "What? That's my husband. He's hurt."

Thomas brought his pistol up to line up a shot on the obviously infected man, but the woman stepped into the line-of-sight and Thomas yelled at her, "Get back! He's infected!"

The lady turned towards Thomas with a look of confusion on her face and said, "Infected? With that SARS stuff?" Then she noticed the gun pointed towards them and started, "Hey, why are you pointing a gun a..."

She was abruptly cut off as her husband grabbed her hair from behind and pulled her off her feet towards him. Her head hit the pavement with a very loud crack and her husband dropped onto her slamming his fists into her face over and over.

Thomas pulled the trigger and blew the man's brains all over his now dead wife.

5.

Thomas sat on his couch in front of a muted television and cradled his head in his hands. It was one thing to see this unfold on television, but it was a whole other thing to experience it firsthand. Thomas had wanted them to take this seriously, and he supposed that wish had been granted, but he was scared that this had gone much further than he had ever anticipated. Thomas only wanted to teach these government leaders a lesson; to make them take infectious diseases more seriously. The lesson he had ended up teaching everyone on the planet was that humans needed to be irradicated. He wasn't sure if he agreed with that message or not, but there was fuck-all he could do about it now.

He thought about the Greek myth of Pandora and how once you release some things into the world they can never be contained again. The thing Thomas had released into the world was death, and it appeared to be insatiable and uncontrollable. It was spreading more invasively than kudzu and was just as unstoppable. At this rate there would be no one left to learn any lesson from what was happening.

Thomas lifted his head out of his hands and his eyes fell onto a photo of his wife on the wall. The photo was from nearly 2 years ago, before she'd gotten sick, and they were out at a cabin in Rock Island. She had been so beautiful; so full of life. They had talked about having a child and their future together that night. It seemed like they had all the time in the world, and nothing could stop them. Twelve months later she was sick and another 4 months after that she was gone.

Thomas' confusion and fear turned back to anger at these thoughts. He remembered learning that he had not only lost his wife, but also his unborn son, and the rage in his heart flared again. Tears of anger and rage flowed down Thomas' cheeks as these thoughts flooded his mind. Thomas thought that deep down he knew how bad this was going to be and that this was exactly what he had really wanted all along. He realized that deep down he didn't feel bad at all that people were dying out in the streets. Thomas hadn't built Pandora's box; he had only opened it to expose what they had put inside it. They created this death, not Thomas. He had simply put their creation on display and let them lay in the bed they themselves made.

Thomas recalled a conversation he'd had with his wife and said aloud, "Thanos wasn't wrong baby. The real disease is humanity... But I think I found a cure."

6.

Thomas heard several explosions over the course of the next 2 hours as he gathered supplies to make the trip he'd decided to make, but only registered them faintly. He knew he probably wasn't going to make it through all this and didn't too much care about that, but he didn't want to die here in this house surrounded by the memories of having to watch his wife slowly choke to death with their unborn child inside her. That would be the worst end to all this that Thomas could imagine.

He had decided to try to get up to Alaska, to the cabin he and Sherry had rented for their honeymoon and make whatever last stand must be made up there. They had enjoyed an amazing week up in that cabin and Thomas couldn't think of a better place to strap in and try to ride this out. Getting there however, was going to be the tricky part.

The roads were all either congested with traffic as people tried to flee the city, or they've been closed off by the military. Thomas needed to fly if he were going to get there and he had the means to do so if he could just get to Murfreesboro and grab the ultralight, he had stored in his friend George's barn. Normally, getting to George's house was just a 35-minute drive, but Thomas knew it was not going to be that easy this time. He had two multiband radios and had tuned one to the state police frequency and the other to the USAF Flight Chief frequency out of Murfreesboro airport while he packed supplies so he could monitor what was truly going on as opposed to the half-truths the media would be showing on the news. The cops were overrun with calls. People were being attacked everywhere by the infected and nearly a quarter of the city was now on fire. The Flight Chief said all commercial traffic had been grounded and that all air traffic was being monitored by the military only.

As he zipped the last backpack of supplies closed, he heard chatter on the Flight Chief frequency, slung the backpack over one shoulder, and stopped to listen. "Lima Bravo 6-4 Charlie, you are in violation of a federal no fly order. Two F-22 Raptors are now on an intercept course with you and will escort you to the Smyrna National Guard airport where you will be boarded and taken into custody. Do you copy?"

There was no reply from the aircraft.

"Lima Bravo 6-4 Charlie, you have been given a direct order by the United States Airforce. Acknowledge or you will be considered hostile."

Still no reply from the plane.

"USAF Flight Chief Murfreesboro, this is F-22 Tango 1 on an intercept with commercial aircraft Lima Bravo 6-4 Charlie, I have a visual on the aircraft," one of the pilots said.

"Copy Tango 1," the Flight Chief responded. "Aircraft has been nonresponsive to radio requests to divert course. Stand by for further orders."

There was a moment of silence and then the Flight Chief came back, "Lima Bravo 6-4 Charlie, please acknowledge and divert course immediately or we will be forced to treat you as a hostile aircraft."

There was only silence.

Finally, the Flight Chief came back and said, "Tango 1, aircraft still unresponsive. Consider aircraft hostile. You are cleared to engage."

There was a long pause and then the pilot responded. "Sir, that's a civilian plane in US airspace."

"I understand Tango 1," the Flight Chief answered. "Aircraft is to be considered hostile. You are clear to engage. Do you copy."

After a short pause the pilot answered, "Copy. Engaging aircraft."

"Lima Bravo 6-4 Charlie, this is F-22 Tango 1, I have missile lock on your aircraft. Please respond and divert course or you will be fired upon."

Silence.

"Tango 1, locked and firing."

"Confirmed hit on target. Target has been neutralized. I repeat, target has been neutralized."

The Flight Chief answered back, "Copy that. Radar confirms target is neutralized. Tango 1, please return to base for debriefing."

"Copy. Tango 1 out."

If Thomas had had any doubts about just how far things had gone, all those doubts had been obliterated by the radio transmission he'd just heard. The US Airforce had just shot down a civilian plane on American soil. Pandora's box was wide open and there was no hope of shutting it now.

Thomas had to move, and he had to move now.

7.

Thomas got behind the wheel of his Dodge Ram 1500 classic and was for once glad he'd bought the oversized gas-guzzling monstrosity. It had been an impulse buy when Thomas had won the Powerball. He'd hit just 6 numbers, but that had been enough to set them up with a house that was paid off and his shiny new truck that was all but useless in Nashville traffic. Now however, that truck was going to ensure that nothing stood in the way of Thomas getting out of this deathtrap of a city and to that cabin in Alaska.

He started the truck before opening the garage door, a thing he would never normally do but which seemed prudent under the circumstances, and then hit the button for the garage door on his visor. He didn't see anyone which was good, but he knew he'd run into people soon enough so he checked his pistol to make sure the safety was off and slid it under his right thigh where he could get to it quickly and easily. He pulled out onto the street and started turning left to get off his street and onto the interstate, when he saw the bodies of the man who had killed his wife, and whom Thomas had subsequently shot in the head, and his dead wife laying in the middle of the street.

There was a moment's pause where Thomas thought about getting out and moving the bodies out of the street, but it was only a moment because Thomas was not risking his life getting out of his truck to move corpses out of the street. He was pretty sure that his truck was tall enough to just drive over them without hitting them, so he proceeded forward. The bump and following squish informed Thomas that although his truck was indeed tall enough to not hit the bodies, his driving skills were not quite good enough to avoid squishing one of them under his rear tire. Thomas hoped it hadn't been one of their heads he'd driven over, but in his heart of hearts he knew it had been.

Thomas stopped at the stop sign at the end of the street and just stared at his teering wheel. During the last 4 hours he'd shot a man who had killed his own wife right in front of him and them run their corpses over with his truck. It was overwhelming. Then the thought occurred to him that, he had actually killed that man's wife too along with every other infected person and every person those infected killed. Thomas realized that he was now the greatest mass-murderer in human history, which was not a title he much cared for.

He looked up from the steering wheel at the city catching fire in front of him. Like it or not, Thomas only had two options; he could either sit here and die to infected or he could push forward and see this thing through as far as he could manage to make it. He looked up into his rearview mirror, back at the house he and his wife had shared for so many years and said a silent goodbye, then stepped on the gas and headed towards George's house and his one chance to get out alive.

8.

Having lived here all his life, Thomas was able to navigate back roads from Nashville to Murfreesboro in a little under an hour, but it had not been an easy ride. Even on the back roads traffic was at an almost crawl, there were at least 10 or more wrecks, and twice Thomas saw an infected attacking people in their own vehicles. Presumably, some had tried to get their sick loved ones out of town and had paid dearly for their efforts. This thing was raging like a fire at an oil derrick.

Thomas got to George's house at a little after 5 am which under any other circumstances would have been an obnoxious time to show up, but Thomas thought that if any time was a good time to shed formalities and politeness in favor of practicality this was that time. He jumped out of his truck and tucked the gun into his waistband at the small of his back and jogged up to George's front door and knocked like the house was on fire, which in a way was sort of true because the whole world was catching fire right now.

There was no answer and Thomas knocked again even more furiously. Still, there was no answer and no lights coming on in the house. Thomas knocked a third time and after another minute without a response he tried the doorknob and found the door unlocked. He opened the door and stepped inside calling out, "Hello? Anybody home? It's Tommy."

No one answered back and Thomas fumbled for the light switch. His finger finally landed on the switch and he flipped it on. The house was in shambles. The furniture was all flipped over, bookshelves were stripped having their books strewn onto the floor, lamps were knocked over or outrightly broken, and even the kitchen was a mess.

There was no way George had done this. Someone had been here, and they'd been looking for something. Considering that George was one of the biggest suppliers of THC concentrates in the area, Thomas had a fairly informed guess as to what they had been looking for. Thomas just hoped that George had not been home when these folks showed up or things could have gotten ugly.

Thinking of that, Thomas realized the intruders might still be here and he immediately pulled his gun and checked that the safety was off. He'd made a lot of noise coming in and whoever had trashed the place might be hiding in wait upstairs or in a closet or something. Thomas moved quietly now to check the coat closet and then the pantry and found them both clear. He walked to the stairs and slowly mad his way up them with the gun at the ready in front of him. The upstairs landing was clear and there were 3 other rooms to clear up here: the bathroom, George's bedroom, and his office. Thomas checked the bathroom and found it empty, but thoroughly tossed then moved to the office. He couldn't even step into the office for the mess on the floor and decided that even if someone were in the closet on the other side of the room, they'd make so much noise getting out and across the room that Thomas would no doubt hear them.

Thomas made his way to the bedroom and opened the door. The room was just as disheveled as the rest, but on the bed lay the body of George Markum. It looked like he had been savagely beaten and then had his throat slit so deeply it nearly took his head clean off. Thomas swallowed back the gorge in his throat and made his way over to check the closet and make sure no one was still here. This task was easy enough as the door was ajar, and Thomas only had to step to that side of the room to see that no one could be hiding there.

Thomas knelt beside his now dead friend and looked at him for a moment.

"What was it you used to say buddy," Thomas queried the corpse? "Play stupid games and win stupid prizes, wasn't it? Let's see if whoever did this to you won the prize they were after."

Thomas reached under the bed and fumbled around blindly for a minute until his hand hit on a little metal box. Thomas gave the box a good tug and it released its magnetic grip from the metal bedframe. Thomas pulled the little box up in front of him and shook it producing a little jingle.

"Bingo," Thomas exclaimed and slid the lid open on the box revealing a key.

Thomas had been the one to suggest this to George 3 years ago when Thomas had been picking up some wax from George. He'd seen that George kept the key to the secure storage shed out back on his keyring and had remarked how careless that was. Thomas had suggested that George get one of those magnetic hide-a-key things you stick under your car from Walmart and putting that key somewhere safe that wasn't on him and wasn't easy to find. Two weeks later Thomas came back over, and George told him he'd done just what Tommy had suggested and even showed Tommy where he was keeping the key.

Thomas looked back down at his now dead friend and said, "You saved my life buddy. I don't know how or why you held out on them, but I'd be right fucked if you hadn't... so thanks. And sorry this happened to ya buddy."

Along with housing tools and old crap George didn't want to throw away, the secure storage shed also held all of George's product and Thomas' ultralight. Thomas got back to his feet, put the gun back in his waistband, and made his way back out of the house. As he came out the front door Thomas saw 2 young guys with baseball bats standing beside his truck.

"Marko!" one of the guys called out and a third guy came walking out from behind the truck.

The third guy smiled viciously and said, "Pollo!"

The third guy had what Thomas recognized at once as a retractable police baton and he smiled even more menacingly while looking at Thomas and said, "Hey mister... maybe you can help me with something. Ya see, the guy who lives here, well, I should say lived here, had something of mine and he couldn't seem to find his way to getting it back to me. You know anything about that?"

Thomas had only been half-listening to this creep's words because he was trying to figure out his next move. He could pull the gun and get at least two of them quick, but he didn't know if any of them also had a gun and he was in no mood to get shot this morning.

"No clue what you're talking about kid," Thomas yelled back. "I just came by to grab a glass of orange juice because I was so thirsty from fucking your mom."

The kid's smile instantly disappeared and was replaced by anger. "What the fuck did you say old man," the guy questioned?

"I said," Thomas responded now smirking, "that I was deep-dicking your mom and the broke skank couldn't afford juice, so I had to come here to get some. She said she dropped you on your head, but I didn't realize it had damaged your hearing."

Thomas never normally talked like that, but he needed to throw this punk off his game to get the upper hand here and this was working perfectly. Alpha male misogyny had never really been Thomas' thing, but sometimes you had to fight fire with fire.

"You fucked up old man," the guy said. "These boys are gonna beat you half-to-death until you tell me where the key to that building is and then I'm gonna chop your fucking head..."

That's as far as the guy got before Thomas pulled his gun and shot the man in the head. The other two goons jumped at the sound of the gunfire and one dropped his bat. The other one dropped his bat and started to reach behind his back when Thomas pulled the trigger again and blew a hole in the guy's chest knocking him back into Tommy's truck and onto the ground. The last guy turned and started to run, and Tommy shot him in the back of the head. Tommy walked over to the guy with a hole in his chest, who was now gurgling up blood and coughing it out and knelt on one knee beside him.

"Normally," Thomas said, "I'm a really nice guy. But you clowns picked the wrong day to fuck with me."

Thomas put the gun against the man's forehead and pulled the trigger. The blood from the man's head splattered back up onto Thomas' face but he never flinched or even moved to wipe it off. As Thomas had been talking to the third man, berating his mother and poverty shaming him, Thomas had realized that there weren't really any rules anymore. He didn't have to worry about explaining to cops why he'd had to kill three people or why he was at the scene of a homicide looking for a key to a shed containing Oden knows how much drugs and other illegal shit because the cops would not be coming, at least not any time soon. And if they did stumble onto this scene after Thomas had left then so what? They couldn't waste manpower looking for him in the middle of all this shit. No, Thomas had decided, there were no rules anymore, and he would do whatever he felt he needed to in order to get where he was going.

Even if that meant killing folks whether they're infected or not and if that made him a murderer then that would be something he alone would have to carry.

Thomas stood back up and walked over to the storage shed. He pulled the key out of his pocket and used it to unlock the four deadbolt locks then threw the key on the ground. It wouldn't do anyone any good anymore. He looked down at the keypad above the doorknob and laughed lightly aloud.

"Those dipshits weren't getting in here even if they had found the key," Thomas mused.

Thomas felt a fresh pang of anger as he punched in the numbers 09-11-11. George had been an EMT in New York when the towers fell and had gotten terribly sick for his heroism. This oh so wonderful government of ours had turned its back on George and hundreds of others after they risked their lives for the citizens of this nation, denying that their illnesses were related to their service for this nation and refusing to provide much needed medical assistance. Thomas had begun losing any faith in the government after that and the problems only escalated as the years went on.

George had been dying and had only started selling the concentrates to pay his medical bills. People think Breaking Bad was just some fantasy television show, but for many folks that's real life. At least, it was. Now, real life is survival at all costs, and if a man will produce and sell illegal drugs just to add a few years onto his life just imagine what he'll do if he must violently struggle just to live through the day. Pretty soon the only survivors left will be those strong enough to kill and still sleep through the night. Thomas didn't know if that was a good thing, but he knew that like it or not that was what was coming.

Thomas opened the door and the motion activated lights came on in the shed. Sitting in the middle was Thomas' ultralight. The glider was sitting propped up in a corner collapsed and would need to be attached, but that was an easy enough job. Thomas walked over to the reinforced garage door in the side wall and pressed the button to raise the door. As the door was raising Thomas walked over to the ultralight to add fuel to the tank from the gas canister on the floor beside a shelf near the vehicle and noticed a large lockbox sitting on the seat of the ultralight. Thomas reached down and picked up the box and saw an envelope laying on the seat underneath the box. He set the box down on the shelf, picked up the envelope, opened it, and pulled out a single tri-folded sheet of paper with a small key taped to the back. He unfolded the paper and read the note written on it.

"Hey buddy. I figured you might be by to get the ride and thought I'd leave this present for ya seeing as I'm heading out first thing in the morning. This shit is crazy man. I'm gonna grab some stuff and try to ride this out on the boat. You're welcome to join me but bring food if you come because I don't have enough for the both of us. There's a pound of THCA wax in the lockbox but remember that it may be the last on earth so don't go crazy on it. No matter what, I hope this all works out and I see ya on the other side of this thing. Peace brother, George."

Damn, Thomas thought, just a few hours away from getting out and these punks come in and slit your damn throat.

"That's some shit luck Georgie boy," Thomas mumbled aloud. "You were a good dude. You didn't deserve to go out like that."

Thomas pulled the key off the note, folded it back closed and in half, and then slid it into his back pocket. He put the key in his front pocket and then picked up the lockbox and carried it back to his truck. He tried to step over one of the bodies of the guys he'd shot earlier to get into his truck but couldn't find enough room for his foot on the far side so he ended up scooting the body over with his foot which any passerby would have been forgiven for thinking was him kicking a dead body out of his way. He got the body moved, opened his truck door, set the lockbox on the passenger seat, and sat down inside. He pulled the key to the lockbox out of his pocket and began to lean over to unlock the box when he noticed his reflection in the rearview mirror and that his face was covered in blood. He reached into the glove box and pulled out the travel package of wet wipes he kept in there and wiped his face clean, checking in the mirror to be sure he'd gotten it all.

Giving himself one last look in the mirror and finding himself presentable again, Thomas leaned over and opened the lockbox to reveal 4 quarter-pound slabs of THCA wax wrapped in wax paper, a nectar collector, a crème brûlée torch, and a can of butane.

"Ho-ly shit," Thomas said to no one in particular as he picked up one of the slabs and held it up to his face.

He sniffed it but there was no smell other than the wax paper. He set the slab back down and picked up the nectar collector and torch because this had been a shitty day and a little hit to relax a bit was due by Thomas' estimation. He pressed the button to light the torch, hoping there was fuel already in it, and it flared to life. He heated up the nectar collector, set down the now extinguished torch, and did a much bigger dab than he had planned. When he exhaled, he thought he would start coughing uncontrollably but it wasn't that harsh at all and he didn't cough too much after all. After about a minute though his forehead started dripping with sweat and his head started spinning.

"Oh shit," he said to no one again and laid his head back on the headrest and closed his eyes. After a few minutes this mellowed out and Thomas took a deep breath then packed all the things from the lockbox into his backpack's front pocket. He grabbed the backpack by the strap and stepped out of the truck and over the dead body beside it.

He reached into his front pocket and produced the keys to the truck, his home, and his storage building, and looked at them for a moment.

"World's gone to shit boys," Thomas said to the corpses laying around the truck. "I'd say it was nice knowing ya but..." Thomas tossed the keys at the corpse he'd shot first, "You got as much use for those as I do now pal."

He turned from the truck and made his way back to the storage shed and slung the backpack into the seat of the ultralight so he could push it out of the building. Thomas pushed the makeshift aircraft outside and then returned in and grabbed the glider. It took him another 20 minutes to get the glider attached by himself, but he managed and was at last almost ready to go. He made one more trip back into the shed to grab the two gas canisters in there, used one to fill the tank of the ultralight and strapped the other to the side compartment of the chassis to refuel later, then sat down on the single step at the door of the shed to rest a minute. He pulled the gun from his back and ejected the magazine to make sure he still had a few shots left, and as he slid the magazine back in, he heard dogs start barking not too far off and then one of those blood-curdling screams followed by dogs yelping.

That was Thomas' que to vacate the premises immediately.

He stood up quickly and jogged back to the aircraft. He strapped his backpack onto the opposite side of the aircraft than the gas canister and then pushed the aircraft into position for taking off from the field in George's back yard and then yanked the chord to start the engine. The engine didn't turn over. Thomas yanked the chord again, but the engine still didn't turn over.

There was another of those screams only closer this time.

Thomas yanked the chord again but still it didn't start.

"Fuck," Thomas said. "I Don't have time for this!"

Another scream came and then Thomas remembered something, "Prime the damn thing dipshit!"

Thomas found the primer pump and pressed it five times just as he remembered from the instructions. It had been over a year since he'd flown this thing and even back when he flew it often, he forgot to prime it many times.

He waited a second after priming, as per the instructions, and then yanked the chord again. The engine roared to life and the large fan on the back spun up into idle.

Another scream, followed by another separate scream, came bellowing out of the dawn darkness and Thomas could tell they were even closer; possibly running towards him. He sat down in the aircraft and strapped into the five-point restraint harness then pushed the throttle lever forward slowly and felt the machine gain speed. He pushed the throttle all the way home and felt the craft lurch off the ground just a bit. He pulled back on the flight stick and the craft began to lift off the ground. Another minute later Thomas was fully airborne and cruising at just slightly above the tree line.

He pulled his phone out of his jacket pocket and slid it into the cradle attached to the craft's chassis and pressed the button to unlock it. There was no service, but GPS was still working and that was all he needed. He had already planned a route and if everything went to plan it would take about 3 days to get to Alaska. He reached into his other jacket pocket and pulled out a protein bar, unwrapped it, and ate it as the sun rose to his back.

Part 2: The Body

The body was starting to smell.

It had only been 16 hours since Kallen had been forced to kill her cellmate but she could swear that the body was already starting to smell. Under normal circumstances a corpse wouldn't manage to sit for 16 hours in a medium security federal prison without being noticed by someone "in charge", but these definitely weren't normal circumstances. Kallen laughed aloud to herself thinking that the worst thing she'd ever done in her life, killing another human being, would be the one terrible thing she'd ever done that she wouldn't be getting caught for having done. She was fairly certain she wouldn't be getting caught for that crime because she was absolutely certain that no one was coming back to this prison. And really... it had been self-defense anyway.

She hadn't seen or even heard a guard in the building in over 4 days at this point and yesterday had been the day her cellmate had snapped and tried to kill her. Kallen had been the only one of the two of them who had commissary and so she had been the only one who had food. She had tried to talk to her cellmate about rationing what she had between the two of them, but twice Kallen had seen her eyeing the locker that held Kallen's possessions with a look that said nothing good was going to come from this. Yesterday Kallen had awakened to a pillow covering her face and her cellmate screaming "die bitch" over and over. Kallen had fought the woman off and had managed to get onto her back. Kallen had wrapped her arm around the neck of her cellmate and proceeded to squeeze until she both heard and felt something pop in the woman's neck and felt the woman go limp in her arms. She had let the woman go and skidded on her butt against the wall at her back. The woman had turned her face towards Kallen and her eyes had been blinking fast, obviously in terrible fear. She had been making a horribly disturbing gurgling sound from her throat. The woman had coughed out a spray of blood which had splattered across Kallen's face and then her eyes went blank.

Kallen had never even seen someone die in person, much less ever killed anyone, and she wasn't sure how she should feel. The woman had tried to kill her. What else could she have done? She supposed she could have just knocked the woman out and then tied her up, but what if she got loose while Kallen was asleep? She couldn't have afforded to take that chance even if she had wanted to, but that was actually a non-point because Kallen's adrenaline had been pumping so hard that she hadn't really had any control over how hard she had squeezed the woman's neck. She had simply wrapped her arm around the woman's neck like she'd seen in movies and then squeezed as hard as she could. She hadn't intended to kill the woman. It had just happened in the heat of the exchange. Even if she were to be found out for this, no one would ever convict her of murder. Involuntary manslaughter maybe; but not murder.

At this point none of that mattered at all because Kallen was trapped in an eight by ten box that was specifically designed to keep people from getting out and the only people with the key that could free her hadn't been seen in days. These people weren't just her jailors; they were also her caretakers in the most literal sense because they provided the food, provided laundering equipment, provided shower access, and pretty much everything else that a person needs to live. For now, the water was still running and Kallen still had food, but she knew those things would run out and she had no idea what she would do when that happened.

And the body was really starting to smell.

Kallen had laid the body on a sheet and had dumped two full bottles of baby powder on it before wrapping it up in the sheet and pushing it under the bottom bunk. She had thought, "Out of sight; out of mind," but that was much easier said than done. Kallen had sworn she could smell the body starting to rot last night, even though she knew that couldn't possibly be true. Kallen hadn't really slept at all. She couldn't stop smelling a smell that she knew wasn't really there... at least, it wasn't really there yet. But that smell would be coming and as far as Kallen's mind was concerned it was already there in the room with her.

She needed to get her mind off of that body. She considered working out but then remembered her food situation and thought better of it. She couldn't afford to burn unnecessary calories. What she needed to do; what her very life depended on her doing, was to figure out how the hell to get out of this goddamn cell. The walls were six feet thick cinderblock with rebar and concrete poured into it that it would take a jackhammer to get through and the door was at least three inches thick of pure steel. The window, if you could even call it that, was specifically designed to be too small to even get a human head through. All those bars and skeleton key jail days were a thing of the past and had been replaced with thick concrete, rebar, steel, and razor-wire. Getting out of the cell itself would only be a start because she would need to still get out of the prison itself.

On top of all that, Kallen was pretty afraid of what could have happened out in the real world that would have made all the guards and staff just abandon this place. She knew the vast majority of the citizens in this country wrote off anyone convicted of a crime the moment the guilty verdict was read, many even before a verdict is read, but they wouldn't just leave everyone in here to starve to death. The government wouldn't just let this happen which meant that there was something very wrong in the government and whatever had happened had been bad and it had been quick. The last thing they'd seen on the news before the whole prison had been put on lockdown was something about some minor infection that had hospitalized some folks. The next day the lockdown had come and then there had only been three more shifts of guards coming around to pass out food before they stopped showing up.

It only took another 12 hours before the fighting broke out. Once they'd failed to feed everyone twice the yelling had started and it only took about an hour before the cellmates of the yellers got sick of the yelling and had started fighting. That had been when Kallen was absolutely sure that no one was going to be coming for them. If they hadn't come to feed them, and they hadn't come to stop them from fighting, then they wouldn't be coming at all.

Kallen had avoided the yelling and the fighting by giving her cellmate some ramen when lunch didn't show up and then another and a honey bun when dinner didn't show up. She hadn't made it this long in here without any major fights or issues by being numb to which way the wind was blowing. She had circled-in on the fact that lunch wasn't coming about 45 minutes after it should have arrived and she immediately realized the only way she would be eating in peace would be to feed her cellmate as well. It was either that or kill the woman and she had no intention of doing that.

Intention or not, the woman had gone from being Kallen's cellmate to being The Body at Kallen's hands. Kallen could only think of her as The Body now. She knew the woman's name. It had been Sherry... or Cherrie. Some shit like that. Or was it Carry? To be honest she hadn't cared for the woman and had only been cellmates with her for the last 5 months. She had been an uninteresting nondescript terribly ignorant woman who had no interest in chatting and nothing worth listening to when she spoke.

Maybe it was Kathy? No. That wasn't it, and honestly it didn't matter. She was dead and now she was just The Body. And nobody was coming for Kallen or for Sherry, Carry, or Kathy or whatever the fuck The Body's name actually was because something was really, really, wrong.

And The Body... The Body was really starting to smell.

She needed to get out of this cell and away from that smell. She had enough food to last at least 3 weeks if she rationed everything out just right, but she would go absolutely insane long before then if she couldn't get away from that goddamn smell. That putrid sweet smell of rot was stronger than anything she could use to try and cover it up. The best thing she had figured out to kill the smell off even a bit was to put a swipe of deodorant right up on her upper lip, but even that only worked so well and only for so long. And after a while that smell would get so bad that nothing would cover it up.

Kallen went to the cell door and yelled out. "Hello! Is anyone else there?!"

No one yelled back so Kallen yelled out again even louder, "Hello!"

Still nothing.

"Guards," Kallen yelled. "I killed my cellie! Bitch attacked me so I killed her! The Body smells!"

For a few minutes Kallen heard nothing, but then she swore she could hear faint laughter.

"Hello," Kallen called out questioningly. "Is someone else there?"

The laughter grew louder and then a hoarse voice called back, "The body," the voice started and then broke into laughter again before continuing, "the body smells! You're damn right the body smells! But it doesn't taste half bad!"

The laughter grew louder and more insane and Kallen backed away from the door. The voice cackled out again, "The body smells, but it tastes, so, damn, good!"

Kallen climbed up onto the top bunk and covered her head with her pillow hoping to drown out the laughter. Kallen regretted having called out at all and hoped that the deranged cannibal down the cellblock would get tired of laughing and shut the fuck up. Kallen laid there, pillow pulled tightly around her head, and pleaded with every god she'd ever been told about and didn't believe in to just make the cannibal shut up.

The next thing Kallen remembered she was waking up unsure of what time it was, but it was dark out and the cannibal had finally shut up so it had to have been several hours. In any case, Kallen was glad for the silence and sat up in the bunk throwing her feet over the side and then froze. Kallen was sure she heard a moan. She sat stalk still for several more minutes and when she didn't hear it again, she hopped down out of the bunk and was immediately struck in the face by the smell. She lurched to the toilet and threw up everything left on her stomach which thankfully wasn't that much given her rationing.

As she was leaned over the toilet, she heard another moan and shoved herself away from the toilet backing herself against the cell door. The moan had come from under the bottom bunk. It had come from The Body. Kallen was scared, but fear had never slowed her down or stopped her so she pulled herself up and was again immediately hit by the smell and nearly threw up again. Then there was another moan and what sounded like a fart and then a blast of that smell hit Kallen like a brick and she lurched to the toilet again with nothing but bile left in her stomach.

The moaning hadn't been moaning at all. The Body was decomposing and gasses were leaking out making these noises and spreading that goddamn smell all over the cell. Kallen ran to the little window and shoved her face as far into the window as she could trying to breath in fresh air. The air was fresher and far more breathable, but Kallen noticed that sickly smell mixed into the air all around her and realized that the whole prison was now a graveyard. The prison was now a graveyard that she was buried alive in.

Kallen started screaming out the window, "Hello! Anybody! I'm trapped in here! Help!!!!"

No one called back, but Kallen did hear what sounded like the sound of a terribly vicious animal and it wasn't far away. As Kallen was about to scream out again a voice came from behind her, "Hey there tasty!"

Kallen swung around and there was a face in the window of her cell door. The face of the woman in the window was clearly insane and was streaked with blood.

The woman in the window smiled at Kallen and said, "Hey sweet meat! Thought I'd come down here and say hello. Do you know how long it takes to unscrew safety screws using just some finger bones?"

Kallen didn't answer. She was too shocked. This woman got out of her cell.

"Two days," the crazy woman said not waiting for a response. "But I think I can get yours done in less than one."

Kallen could hear scraping at her door and then the woman brought something up beside her face and Kallen could see it was a bone.

"Got a bigger bone this time," the cannibal said. "Just gimme a little time sweet meat. I'll get in there soon enough. Gotta eat sweet meat. Gotta eat."

The face disappeared out of the window and Kallen could hear her working at the screws of the door. Kallen's back was against the window of her small cell and even though there was a psychotic cannibal attempting to break into her cell, Kallen's main thought was the goddamn smell from The Body. If the psycho got the door open that might actually be a plus. Kallen was pretty sure she'd rather fight a psychotic cannibal than go insane from that fucking smell. Kallen's stomach churned and she dry-heaved slightly but choked it back and composed herself. She opened her locker box and grabbed the deodorant stick that was nearly completely gone and rubbed nearly all the rest of the stick onto her upper lip which settled her stomach enough for her to be able to think.

She pushed her face into the window again and drew in the fresher air and then turned back to her locker. She stared inside trying to figure out what her play was. She wanted the cannibal to get into the cell because if she could get in then Kallen could get out. The problem was what to do once the woman got in. Kallen wasn't a killer despite what had caused The Body to be under the bottom bunk. This woman on the other hand did not seem to be new to this concept and she was starving. Given that Kallen was this woman's food source, Kallen figured she would be coming in with everything she had.

As Kallen stared into her locker trying to figure this out her eyes settled on four bottles of baby oil. A memory came to mind of a story her ex had told her about his time in prison.

"So, I'm in the hole," he had said, "and they still want me to dress out for inspection and get out of bed, but I'm like fuck that so I tell them I'm not doing it and they threaten to send in the riot goons and I tell them to kiss my ass. So, I know they're gonna send these big asshole riot guards in on me and I strip down butt-ass naked and I grab these bottles of baby oil out of my locker and start spraying it all over myself and the floor of my cell and just wait on these dicks to come in. They open the cell door and as soon as the first one steps in, he slips and I just kick him right in the chest like some 300 shit and send him flying back out of the cell."

The story had continued and in the end the guards had thrown in teargas on him and he'd gotten his ass beaten, but the important part was the first part. There weren't any guards to teargas Kallen anymore and she only had to deal with one crazy cannibal bitch. She pulled the baby oil out of the locker and put it on the shelf. She had a plan. Granted it was only the beginnings of a plan, but that was better than nothing.

"Fuck," Kallen said to The Body. "You smell so goddamn bad! Why couldn't you just be cool and we could deal with Crazy the Cannibal together and get the fuck out of here? You fucking suck Body and you smell so terrible. Fuck you Body!"

Kallen stuck her head in the window again and took a breath.

"You're not the only thing that's rotten here in Denmark dear stinking Body," Kallen said to The Body. "We're trapped in a cemetery stinky Body and only one of us is dead. Gonna have to dig my way out through a psychotic cannibal you putrid Body you, but make no mistake that I will dig through because your stench is fucking unbearable and I'll go insane if I don't get away. It's nothing personal Body."

"Who you talking to sweet meat," the crazy lady asked with her head cocked to one side in the cell door window again?

"Just talking to The Body crazy lady," Kallen said.

"More sweet treats," the crazy lady questioned?

"That treat is spoiled you fucking fruit bat," Kallen replied with a laugh.

The lunatic hit the door and growled at Kallen and then her face disappeared again and the working on the screws started back up. Kallen looked back into the locker and saw the baby powder behind some chips. She grabbed the chips and threw them up onto her bunk and then grabbed the baby powder. Kallen lifted the bottom mattress off of the bottom bunk and started shaking the baby powder like crazy over The Body under that bunk. She shook that baby powder until it ran out and then threw the empty container into the corner and laid the mattress back over the bunk. She jumped up onto her bunk and opened up the bag of chips. She did her best to both eat and hold her breath at the same time which was quite difficult but she needed to eat.

Kallen was tired, but she didn't dare temp sleep with crazy ass Hannibalina out there weaseling her way in here. Kallen figured her lunatic friend outside was getting close to getting in because she had started giggling a bit frantically. Kallen hopped down off her bunk and grabbed the bag of Keefe instant coffee out of her locker and scooped a spoonful into her mouth, took a swig of water from the open water bottle on the shelf, and swished it all around in her mouth then swallowed hard. She did this once more and then washed it down with another sip of water. She shivered as the caffeine hit her system with a jolt that widened her eyes and got her feeling a bit more awake.

Kallen didn't drink coffee or sodas much at all so when she had caffeine, especially as much as she had just taken in, she felt it very strongly. She closed her eyes and let the caffeine do its job to reenergize her and she centered herself for what was coming. She'd had to fight for her life more times than she liked to think about but she was still here which meant she must be pretty good at it. She wasn't sure if it was a misfortune or a privilege to have had the experiences, she'd had that had made her so strong, but in this moment, she was pretty sure she was at least lucky to have some experience.

Kallen opened her eyes and stripped out of her jumpsuit and into her birthday suit then proceeded to start covering herself and the floor of the cell in baby oil. She threw the empty bottles into the corner of the cell and braced one foot against the back wall of her cell and stared forward at the cell door.

After a few minutes Hannibalina popped her face back into the window of the cell door. The mad woman held up a screw and smiled. "Got the last one sweet meat. It's time to eat."

Kallen smiled back at the lunatic in the window and said, "I have been told I'm quite the snack lady. Come get some."

The crazy woman jerked the cell door's handle and the entire handle and lock mechanism fell out of both sides of the door. Hannibalina kicked the door and it flew open hitting the toilet and sink combo behind it. The lunatic screamed and started to lurch forward at Kallen. She slipped on the baby oil and started windmilling her arms as she began falling backwards and Kallen pushed off of the wall behind her with one foot and jumped up to bring both of her knees directly into the lunatic's chest and send her flying back out of the cell. Kallen landed on the floor with a hard thud that knocked the breath out of her.

Kallen sat up and tried to take in a breath which hitched in her throat. She could see the lunatic out on the catwalk outside her cell trying to catch her breath and get back onto her feet as well. Then

Kallen heard something that sounded like a freight train coming right at her. She looked around trying to figure out what that sound was and where it was coming from and then realized it was coming from above them to the west. Kallen looked out of the cell doorway into the common area and could see a bright light coming in through the skylights. Kallen got to her feet and backed up to the wall again as that sound grew louder.

The lunatic caught her breath and her eyes met Kallen's. The lunatic screamed and scrambled onto her feet meaning to run in on Kallen again and totally oblivious to the sound and lights bearing down on them. Kallen however was acutely aware of that sound and those lights and she grabbed her mattress off of her bunk and threw it over herself with less than a second to spare before the Boeing 747 crashed into cellblocks C and D along with the front gate.

Kallen came to several hours later, although she had no idea just how long she had been unconscious, and was immediately hit by the most horribly sharp pain she had ever felt in her life shooting through her thigh. That pain was a result of the large shard of metal that was also shooting threw her thigh. She wanted to scream but life had taught her over the years that screaming was often the worst option when pain in any form came calling and so she winced in a deep breath through her teeth instead. She looked down at her thigh and twisted herself slightly to try and see if the metal went all the way through her leg or if it was attached to anything on the other side. Luckily the metal was a singular shard that had broken off of something, whether the plane or some other item from within the prison Kallen didn't know, and if she was extremely lucky it hadn't hit her femoral artery.

Kallen lifted her thigh wincing hard as she did and grabbed the metal shard from the backside of her thigh as that was the larger side of the object and she pulled slightly on it to see how much blood came out and she held in a stifled scream as she did but her eyes stayed steadily trained on watching the blood flow and she saw that it was minimal.

In this moment, Kallen was extremely aware and quite upset that she was naked because she could really use some sort of cloth to stop the bleeding when she pulled this goddamn thing out. Kallen looked around for the first time since regaining consciousness and she saw Hannibalina's face, eyes completely blank and quite obviously devoid of any life, and could see that a cinderblock had gone clean through the back of her skull. At least that problem had resolved itself.

Kallen reached out and grabbed the psychotic woman's shirt and pulled hard hoping to rip a large piece of cloth from the woman's shirt but when she yanked on the shirt, the woman's entire torso came loose from the rest of her body which was buried under the ruble of a wall and blood sprayed across Kallen's face and chest which startled the hell out of her. The blood startled her because she was sure that once a person's heart stopped beating that this sort of blood spray wouldn't happen. Bile rose in Kallen's throat and she nearly threw up but she choked it back. She closed her eyes for a moment and took a deep breath and then the smell of The Body hit her nostrils and she couldn't hold back the bile this time and projectile vomited directly onto what was left of Hannibalina's face.

"Fuck," Kallen hissed. "That fucking smell! How the hell is that smell still so damn strong?"

Kallen felt bile rise in her throat again, but she steeled herself and grabbed the shirt of the psycho which still had a torso in it, grabbed both sides of the shirt, ripped it open, and jerked the arms out of the shirt. She shoved the body away and ripped the shirt in half which took a lot more force than she thought it would. She laid both halves of the shirt over her chest and then reached down and grabbed the metal shard in her thigh again. She took a breath, nearly threw up again, held her breath, and then jerked the shard out of her thigh and screamed into her own throat and mouth. Kallen's eyes opened wider than they ever had in her life and she exhaled all the breath left on her lungs. She breathed in again, The Body being the only smell she could smell in all the world, and she fought with all her strength not to throw up again. She grabbed one half of the shirt draped over her chest and ripped two smaller pieces off of it. She balled up the two smaller pieces of cloth and winced as she shoved them into the two holes in either side of her thigh and then tied the rest of that half of the shirt around the rather large hole in her thigh and yanked the cloth tight in a knot around her thigh.

Kallen laid her head down on the ruble underneath her and closed her eyes letting the pain course through her body like jolts of electricity washing over her and just tried to blend into the pain like she always had when she'd been injured in some way. She thought about that book she had been reading, the one about the kid who became a king of that desert planet, and how he'd been put through that fear test and had recited some mantra about letting the fear pass over and through him and how only he would remain and Kallen tried to do the same with the pain she was feeling now. It was mind over matter. She focused her mind on trying to convince herself that the pain didn't matter and after several minutes Kallen opened her eyes again and just stared up into the sky.

As she laid there trying to work up the strength to pick herself up and try to get out of that damn prison, Kallen heard a scream that shot a whole new type of fear into her, like something out of a damn horror movie, and she shot up into a sitting position so fast it sent fresh pain shooting through her thigh and a whole new pain throbbing into her head. That first scream was followed by two more and Kallen's eyes shot around to try and place which direction the sounds had come from but couldn't quite place it. Another of those screams came, this time from closer and most definitely from behind her and to the left behind the prison.

She wasn't waiting around to figure out who or what was making that sound and she summoned all the strength she could to push herself up onto her feet. The pain in her thigh was excruciating, but the leg was holding her weight, and she had by her estimation overstayed her welcome at this oh so posh establishment, so she took a few tentative steps forward. She stumbled once, caught herself, and then started trying to find a way through all the ruble and out of the prison. She took a step forward onto a section of wall in front of her and heard a squish sound while simultaneously being hit in the face like a ton of bricks with the smell from The Body. That smell hit Kallen so hard she lurched forward throwing up the large abundance of nothing left on her stomach which ended up being more of a terrible lurching dry-heave with a miniscule fraction of pure stomach bile so rich in acid it burned her whole esophagus as it came up.

"Jesus fucking Christ," Kallen yelled at The Body. "The fucking walls come down and you're still here just fucking up my day. I swear to fuck I'd kill you again and I didn't even mean to do it the first time. I'm getting out of this shithole and away from your fucking stench. I hate you and I hate this place and I'm pretty sure the whole world has gone to shit, but I'm getting the fuck out of here and I'm going to live. Fuck you stupid ass Body."

Kallen started walking again and slowly made her way to what was left of the mangled gates that had been keeping her locked away from the free world. As she stepped over those fallen gates a mad smile came to Kallen's lips as she thought about what she would look like if anyone was around to see her right now walking naked out of a wrecked prison with half a shirt wrapped around a gaping hole in her thigh and dried gory viscera splattered across her chest and face. That smile disappeared in a flash as another of those inhuman screams came bellowing out from behind her.

Kallen had no idea what was making that sound and she was sure she didn't want to find out, but running was kind of out of the question in her current condition. She needed a safe place to hunker down and try to fix the hole in her leg, but she would settle for a car with at least half-a-tank of gas and the keys in them. The chances of that happening where exactly zero though, and she was very aware of this. Nevertheless, the parking area for the guards was only about 30 yards out from the front gates and Kallen could see several cars still there, so that was her current destination. Even if there wasn't a car with keys in it just queued up waiting on her over there, she could at least maybe scavenge up some clothes or a coat; hell, even a blanket if the universe decided to smile at her. At the very least, she might could find a car with an unlocked door that she could climb into the back seat of and sleep until sun-up to try and gain some strength.

Kallen shambled over the debris, cutting her feet on a mixture of concrete ruble, safety glass, and metal shards as she did so, all while cussing and hissing with every step. She finally managed to reach the concrete of the parking area and took a minute to sit on the warden's bumper and pick as much trash out of her feet as she could see in the feeble light of a near fully obscured moon. She timidly put her feet back onto the pavement and slowly leveraged her weight off of the car and onto her feet which still stung but now hurt far less and didn't feel as though new pain was being ground into them with every step so that was better. Kallen stood still for a few moments and steeled herself to continue on into the lot and to let a messed-up thought bounce around in her mind.

"Lot of goddamn cars in this lot for a prison that hasn't had a guard walking around in a fucking week," Kallen said aloud to herself. "Wonder what had to happen to make these fuckers just abandon all of us and all of their shit."

As Kallen took a step forward, another of those inhuman screams came from the woods about 20 yards away across from the prison and Kallen's eyes shot towards the sound. Kallen stumbled forward a step or two, tripped on something laying across the ground in front of her, and reached out to catch herself on the car in front of her. She looked down to see what she had tripped over and saw an arm that was sleeved in a guard's uniform. The arm was missing the rest of the body it should be attached to and Kallen immediately thought that she'd seen far more dismembered body parts in the last few hours than she had ever thought she would see and more than she had ever wanted to see.

Another scream issued out, this time much closer, and Kallen pushed herself back upright and started walking as fast as she could not knowing exactly what she was trying to get to and then something caught her eye. Was that... yep. It was an ambulance. That was probably the best thing Kallen could see at this moment and was now the most important thing in Kallen's life. She shuffle-walked, an almost skip-like gesture that Kallen thought would look hilarious to anyone who saw it if anyone had been around to see it, that was only slightly faster than a basic walk.

Another of those screams came, way too close for Kallen's liking, and Kallen swung her head in the direction of the scream and saw what looked like either a short woman or a young teenager running towards the parking lot. Kallen shuffled faster towards the ambulance and was about 10 feet short of the large van when she tripped again and had just enough sense still left to her to try and roll as she fell as not to fall directly on her face and injure herself even further. Kallen landed hard on her side, thankful immediately that she had landed on her leg that didn't have a huge hole in it, but she still hit the ground very hard.

"Fucking hell," Kallen hissed at herself and started pushing herself back up onto her feet and stopped short staring back towards her feet. She had tripped over a shotgun. She grabbed the weapon and got to her feet. She was fixing to check the gun for shells when she heard something slam into the remaining fencing to her left and looked over just as, what was now obviously a young teenage girl, issued another of those inhuman screams and Kallen could see no humanity left in the girl's face. The girl's eyes were beyond bloodshot. They looked pure black, but Kallen knew that couldn't be right. Either way, Kallen did not want to have to deal with another psychotic person trying to kill her.

The girl at the fence pulled as if trying to yank the fence down, and for the first time since she had been booked at the county jail over 2 years ago, Kallen was actually glad there was a fence between her and the outside world. Kallen got back to shuffling to the ambulance, a very sick young woman screaming out at her the whole way, and noticed that the makeshift bandage around her injured leg was soaked through with blood and that blood was now running far faster down her leg than was acceptable. Kallen needed to get to that damn ambulance and she needed for it to not be completely looted or whatever. She didn't know what had happened, and honestly at this point she didn't really give a rat's ass, but whatever had happened meant that there was no one who could help her and if she was going to survive for even another hour, she would have to help herself.

Just as Kallen reached the ambulance the girl at the fence behind her screamed out again and Kallen jerked her head in time to see that the girl had been pacing her along the fence and had come to a spot where someone had apparently wrecked a car through the fence and the girl had climbed over the trunk of this car and was now sprinting directly at Kallen faster than Kallen had ever seen anyone run before.

"What the fuck," Kallen said as she raised the shotgun, "is wrong with everyone lately?"

Kallen pulled the trigger and was greeted with the click of an empty chamber followed by an especially violent young girl who was screaming like some demon slamming her entire body into Kallen whose back then slammed into the ambulance. The girl tried to bite Kallen in the face, but Kallen had managed to keep her grasp on the shotgun lodging the weapon between the two of them and giving Kallen just enough leverage to keep from having her face bitten off. Kallen felt a burst of deep anger fill every nerve of her body. Kallen pushed herself off of the ambulance using her ass and pushed the shotgun in her hands hard into the chest of the girl trying to eat her face while also throwing her entire body weight onto the girl like a raging spider monkey with a shotgun.

The girl hadn't even tried to stop herself from falling backwards as Kallen threw herself onto the girl, seeming fully transfixed on eating Kallen's face and absolutely oblivious to everything else, and when she hit the pavement with Kallen's full weight and momentum pushing her down the girl's head hit the pavement with a crunch. Not a crack. A crunch. Like a walnut being crushed in a nutcracker. This did not however, stop the girl's mouth from snapping several more times before Kallen mustered up a bit more strength and brought the butt of the shotgun down hard on the girl's face.

Kallen pushed herself up onto her feet and grabbed the barrel of the shotgun in both hands and then swung the butt down like a makeshift axe onto the girl's skull one more time and crushed what was left of her head. The body of the girl twitched and Kallen threw the shotgun at it.

"Fuck," Kallen took a breath, "you," she took another breath almost panting, "fucking," she panted twice more, "cannibal bitches."

Kallen wanted to sit down, wanted to lay down, but she didn't dare let herself stop moving right now. If she stopped moving, she might just run out of any ability to move at all. She pulled at the handle of the back doors of the ambulance and felt it locked tight.

"That adds up," Kallen said to herself. "Let's try door number two."

Kallen shambled around to the driver's side door and tried the handle. Locked.

"Swing and a miss," Kallen lilted to herself with a slight laugh and realized that she might have actually lost a bit more blood than was healthy for normal human living and for clear and concise thinking. Kallen shuffled around the front of the ambulance, leaning her weight heavily on the ambulance the whole time, and grabbed the handle of the passenger side door.

"Third time's a charm," she said with a giggle and pulled the handle. The door came open toward Kallen and she nearly fell on her ass because she had been holding more of her weight on the door than she'd realized, but she pulled herself back towards the door and flung out her other hand onto the side of the ambulance to catch herself.

"Yes mufucker," Kallen said to the ambulance looking up and seeing that the interior light had come on and pulled herself into the passenger seat. She pulled the door shut and hit the lock. She leaned her head back on the seat, closed her eyes, and took a deep breath. After a second Kallen's eyes shot open and she said, "nope."

She took another deep breath and then said, "Gotta keep moving."

She reached up above her head and fumbled her hand around until she found the interior dome light and switched it on. She twisted herself in the seat and got onto her knees in between the seats and into the back of the ambulance. She reached up and grabbed the front edge of the gurney in the back and pulled herself into a hunched standing posture. She walked herself around the side of the gurney and sat down on it once she'd reached the middle. She looked up and scanned the ceiling of the ambulance and finally saw the light switch. She hit the light switch and immediately slammed her eyes shut and one hand over them.

"Jesus that's bright," Kallen said as she blinked her eyes behind her hand trying to get them to adjust to the light. Her head was starting to swim and she had to get this blood loss under control immediately or she was going to pass out and bleed to death. She squinted her eyes and scanned the cabinets lining the sides of the back of the ambulance and her eyes finally fell on a medium size bag that was strapped onto the side of the ambulance underneath one of the shelves. She grabbed the bag and tried to pull it off the wall towards her and nearly pulled herself off of the gurney instead because she hadn't realized how strong the hook and loop straps were that were holding it to the wall.

"Fuck me with a cactus," Kallen spat at the bag. "I just need some stitches and gauze you damn stupid bag! Is that so much to ask for huh? Just wanna close up the large hole in my leg and then pass out in the hopes that this is all just a psychotic break and I'm gonna wake up in a strait jacket somewhere tomorrow. Now stop fucking with,"

Kallen stopped talking and her breath lurched in her throat as bile rose. That smell. How the hell was that smell in here? The Body was buried under a goddamn wall over 100 yards away. There was no way that smell was still here... and yet, at least as far as her nose was concerned, that fucking smell was right here and stronger than ever. Kallen threw up bile into her own mouth, but choked it back down her throat and forced herself to take a breath.

"I'm not bleeding to death in this goddamn ambulance in a fucking prison parking lot," Kallen yelled at herself. She reached out and yanked at the straps fastening the bag to the wall and jerked the bag by the handle to her and it fell into her lap. She pulled it off her lap and onto the gurney beside her and then unzipped it and started yanking stuff out until she came across a bunch of gauze pads, two gauze wraps, and what Kallen was pretty sure was a staple gun for stapling humans closed. She pushed the bag off the gurney and then pulled her legs up onto the gurney.

Kallen untied the makeshift bandage around the hole in her leg and her head started swimming. She winced and closed her eyes tight trying to force the spinning to stop and after a few moments she felt centered and slightly more clear-headed. She opened her eyes and, "Oh fuck," she blurted out as bile tried to leap out of her stomach via her throat and she slammed her hand across her mouth so she didn't puke on her own lap. Kallen's eyes darted around the ambulance again and finally fell on what she thought would fix the problem. She grabbed the oxygen mask from off of the tank behind her left shoulder and put it over her nose and mouth and then turned the handle at the top of the tank. Oxygen started coming through the mask and Kallen took a deep breath and her eyes widened.

Kallen's brow furrowed as confusion and anger came to her as the smell of The Body was still there even with an oxygen mask on. That couldn't be real which meant Kallen was losing her fucking mind. She closed her eyes and said aloud to herself, "Get your shit together dumbass," and then opened her eyes.

Kallen started to pull the shirt pieces she'd used to pack into the hole through her thigh and then realized she hadn't grabbed anything to disinfect or clean the damn hole with. "Fucking hell," she cussed at herself and then leaned off the gurney and grabbed the bag again rummaging through it and finally falling on a bottle of betadine. She righted herself sitting back up on the gurney and huffed at herself, annoyed that she couldn't seem to get her mind working.

She picked up the staple gun tool and examined it for a few seconds closely just to make sure she understood, or at least thought she understood, how to use the thing. It seemed simple enough really. It was shaped like a gun with a squeeze trigger and a pincer at the tip. The obvious use process seemed like it would be to pinch the skin together that she needed to keep together and then press the pincer tip to the skin and squeeze the trigger.

"Easy peezy," Kallen said holding the staple gun up in front of her face again, "lemon squeezy," she finished and squeezed the trigger. A staple popped out of the pincer end and Kallen raised an eyebrow thinking that this was going to hurt every single time she had to staple. "Welp," she said and cocked her head to the side a bit, "let's get this done."

Kallen sat the staple gun down beside her and unwrapped the makeshift bandage around her thigh, then pulled the shirt-piece waddings out of the holes on either side. Blood flowed heavily from the wound and Kallen opened one of the gauze pads, doused it in betadine, and cleaned both sides of the hole as best as she could stand to given the immense pain she was starting to feel far more fully as the oxygen served to clear her head more than she was happy about. She figured it would be best to start with the hole on the outer-side of her thigh than the inner one because that one was a bit harder to get to so she leaned the knee of her injured leg in towards the wall of the ambulance on the other side. She took a deep breath, The Body still present in her nostrils with every breath but now being a background thought in anticipation of the upcoming self-surgery, and pinched the hole in her thigh shut as well as she could.

Kallen's eyes shot wide and she clinched her lips together to keep from crying out. What did rise behind those lips was that sound you make when you stub your toe late at night and don't want to wake everyone else in the house screaming. It was a sort of hum-scream-laugh, "Hmmm-mmmmm-hhhhhmmm-mmm."

She picked up the staple gun and pressed the pincer end to the furthest edge of the squeezed together hole in her thigh and squeezed the trigger. This was followed by Kallen slamming the hand holding the staple gun down hard on the gurney beside her and a far stronger hum-scream-laugh that had lost any laughter. She took several deep breaths, squeezed the wound together again which sent fresh waves of pain through her, pulled the staple gun back up to the wound a few centimeters from the first staple, and pulled the trigger again. Another stifled hum-scream, no laugh, rocked Kallen's body and throat and tears started at the corners of Kallen's eyes.

She knew she couldn't stop, no matter how bad it hurt, so she took a few more deep breaths and continued. Another squeeze. Another staple. Another stifled hum-scream. This continued for a total of fifteen staples, six on the exit wound side and nine on the entry side, but the tears had stopped after staple number three. Kallen hadn't ever been much for producing tears or for sadness in general and had always tended more towards being angry rather than being sad. In this moment Kallen wasn't sad that this was happening; she was angry that it was happening to her because she didn't deserve this shit. She wasn't some badass killer criminal. She was just a forgettable grifter running bank fraud cons stealing federally insured money.

Kallen opened another gauze pad package and used the gauze and betadine to clean her surgical handiwork and then opened two more gauze pads and laid one on the outside wound covering it. She opened the gauze roll package and partially unrolled the gauze starting it from the outside of her thigh to hold the gauze pad in place and began winding it around her thigh. She held the first end over the gauze and used her other hand to place the other gauze pad on the other wound on the inside of her thigh and then used her thumb and birdie finger to hold them in place while she used her now free hand to grab the gauze roll and get it around and over itself so she could remove her hand holding the gauze pads in place. She got it started and then wound it as tightly as she could stand to and tucked the last of the roll into the gauze wrapped around her thigh like a post-shower towel around one small section of her thigh.

Kallen swiped all the left-over packaging and crap off of the gurney and laid down on her back. She closed her eyes and just took in steady breaths trying to decide if it was safe to sleep or if she might die if she let herself do so. The Body asserted itself more as Kallen started to regain a true sense of calmness and some respite from the desperation she had been living through for the last week or more. Kallen winced her eyes closed tighter and tried to force her brain to not smell a stench that wasn't actually there. Then Kallen started shivering and became aware once again that she was completely naked and it was actually cold as hell.

Kallen opened her eyes and sat up. There was a thin sheet on the gurney mattress but no blanket. Kallen figured there had to be something in this ambulance, so she started looking through the cabinets again and finally found a package labeled emergency blanket. She opened the package and removed what seemed to be a blanket made from aluminum foil. She pulled it over herself and was surprised that it actually did start to warm her up pretty quickly. Kallen laid over onto her side pulling her knees up slightly into a semi-fetal position and allowed her eyes to close again.

Kallen woke up as bright sunlight made its way in through the back windows of the ambulance and shone directly into Kallen's eyelids. She tried to roll away from the light, her sleep-self not thinking of her terribly damaged thigh, and jerked her eyes open when pain shot through her thigh like she had been freshly stabbed all over again. Kallen's upper body shot into a sitting position and Kallen began to shout, "Motherfuhq," she gagged as the smell of The Body invaded her senses and she rushed forward throwing open the rear doors of the ambulance and spewing bile from her mouth like a scene from The Exorcist.

She tried to take a breath, choked a bit on bile that hadn't fully evacuated her throat, and started coughing so hard that it hurt her throat. After a moment she gained control of herself and was able to get some air into her lungs and was thankful that the air was full of smoke from the plane and prison wreckage several yards away. The smoke, while making breathing much harder, had an acrid smell to it which was in such great supply at the moment that it actually managed to overwhelm the smell of The Body in Kallen's mind.

Kallen got to her feet and stumbled a bit as she put more weight on her bad leg than the leg found acceptable. She managed to get a hand out and grab the open door of the ambulance so she didn't fall. She looked around coughing lightly from the smokey air and then her eyes fell on a car in the row opposite the one the ambulance was parked in two spaces to the right. Kallen could see what looked like someone sitting in the car. Kallen looked down to make sure she didn't trip yet again and saw the shotgun she had used to deal with psycho cannibal number two. She picked up the weapon and didn't bother checking the chamber, instead deciding that the weapon would do more damage if used like a bat.

She grabbed the shotgun by the barrel with one hand and used it as a makeshift cane and walked over to the car. When Kallen was a few feet away she saw the blood splatter on the driver's side rear window and rear windshield along with the hole and spiderwebbed glass of the rear windshield. Kallen approached the car cautiously and tried the driver's side door which came open freely in Kallen's hand and released the smell of this body which had been gaining rank as it sat and which hit Kallen in the face like a physical object rather than an odor.

Kallen erupted bile from herself again and followed this with dry heaves for a solid two minutes, unable to get control of her gag reflex. She finally regained herself enough to reach out and slam the door back shut trying to shut the smell back into the car. It helped, but the smell lingered and intermingled itself with the smell of The Body already burned into Kallen's psyche. Kallen could feel her mind starting to break; could feel her sanity crumbling like the walls of this prison when a fucking passenger jet crashed into it. She knew deep down that no matter where she went or what she did, that smell was going to stay with her. She had escaped a prison of concrete and steel only to walk right into a prison created by her own tortured mind in which her own senses attacked her in perpetuity.

She wanted to just drop onto her ass and start crying and wait on another psycho cannibal to come eat her. If this was life now, she thought she might be better off dead. She almost let this thought win; almost let her knees buckle and herself collapse, but a memory came to her mind and she just stood there for several minutes.

"Why didn't you just dress out and make your bunk baby," Kallen had asked her ex.

He had smiled at her and said, "Because no matter the situation, you can't just let other people dictate your life. You have to fight sometimes; not to prove something to whoever you're fighting, but to remind yourself that your life should be in your hands and if it isn't then it isn't worth living. You fight, even when you know you can't win, because sometimes the universe smiles on you and you win even when you shouldn't."

Kallen took a breath and stood up straight. "You still fighting out there Justin," Kallen asked aloud to the ex-boyfriend who she had no idea was even still alive?

She looked at the car again, "If you're alive you're still fighting," she said taking a step back to the car and reaching her hand out to grab the handle.

"Keep fighting," Kallen said, held her breath, and opened the door.

Kallen saw the nametag saying Brayden and felt a slight sadness. Brayden hadn't been a total tool and all things considered Kallen was pretty sure she hadn't deserved to go out like this and just be forgotten in a prison parking lot. Sad or not however, Kallen needed this woman's clothes and she started stripping them off of the corpse starting with the shoes and working her way up.

It took Kallen over ten minutes to get this done as she tried her best to keep from vomiting, failing to do so three times, but she finally did get the uniform removed from the body. She gathered all the clothes in her arms and got to her feet. She hadn't taken the woman's underwear because that had seemed both wrong somehow and also there was a long-engrained thought that wearing another person's underwear is unhygienic which shouldn't matter to Kallen at this point but still did to her clearly neurotic mind.

Kallen walked back over to the ambulance and climbed into the back again closing the doors behind her. She tossed the clothes on the gurney and looked down at herself. Her whole body was covered in various forms of grime and disgustingness from blood and bile mixed with baby oil to dirt, concrete ruble, and glass also mixed with baby oil. She didn't really just want to drape clothes over filth if she could help it so she riffled through the cabinets again. After several minutes she found two small towels, four more bottles of betadine, and two liters of bottled water.

Kallen took another ten minutes to clean herself as best as she could using these things and honestly felt she was pretty clean aside from her hair which appeared to have been replaced by straw stollen from a scarecrow. Nothing she could really do about that, so she went ahead and got dressed. The clothes were a size too big for Kallen but she was happy to have them regardless. She wasn't really interested in trying to survive whatever was going on with her tits flapping in the wind the whole time.

Kallen sat back down on the gurney and picked up the blister-pack of pills she'd also found while trying to find something to clean herself up with. The package said meperidine and Kallen knew, thanks to a much less pleasant ex-boyfriend, that this was the generic name for Demerol. Her time with that ex informed her that this was a very strong painkiller and Kallen had twenty of them in her hand now. She had never been into drugs much at all other than marijuana and had never been into pills at all. In a past life, she would have considered those pills to be cash just waiting to be collected but in this life, they might be the thing that allows her to keep fighting instead of just falling over in pain and dying.

Kallen popped one of the pills from the blister pack and was about to just pop it in her mouth and swallow when she realized she didn't know what strength these things were and decided she should only take half. She broke the pill in half and swallowed one half while putting the other half into the breast pocket of the uniform shirt for later.

Despite now having clothes, not leaking blood like a busted dam any more, and not being actively attacked by a raging psychotic cannibal, Kallen was still in serious distress. The Body was in her mind and so it was in her nose and it was ripping her brain apart. She had to find some way of making that fucking smell go away. She grabbed the bag off the floor again and rummaged through it until everything in the bag was transferred to the floor. There was nothing in there that could help. She had ransacked the rest of the ambulance and hadn't found anything that could help in any of the cabinets.

"Fuck," Kallen yelled a bit more loudly than she had intended.

Her eyes darted around the ambulance trying to see something she had missed but she didn't see anything. She turned to leave the ambulance through the back and then stopped. The one place she hadn't looked was the glove box. She swirled and took a step to get to the front and her head swam. She steadied herself on the gurney with one hand and stood there for a minute until her head stopped spinning. She needed to eat and let her body replace the blood she'd lost. First however, she needed to check the glove box and then figure out where to go from here. She leaned into the front of the ambulance and opened the glove box.

"Bingo gringo," Kallen exclaimed as her eyes fell on the large jar of vapor cream! Kallen grabbed the jar and screwed the lid off. The jar was almost totally full which put a huge smile on Kallen's face. She took the index and bird finger of her free hand into the cream and scooped a decent size swipe out of the jar and then ran those two fingers directly under her nose. The menthol vapors rose into Kallen's nose and became the only thing Kallen could now smell.

Kallen took a huge deep breath and smiled as the vapor filled her nostrils and she didn't feel her gorge rise in her throat. "Fuck yeah," she said to the empty ambulance.

Kallen got out of the ambulance and was closing the doors behind her when she heard a sound behind her. She turned around quickly and then ran over to the car which had crashed through the fencing and hunkered down in front of the car. The sound she heard was a car, or maybe a truck. As it got closer Kallen became certain it was some sort of truck. Kallen peeked over the hood of the car and out towards the road that was a dead end straight into this prison. She couldn't see the vehicle yet, but the only reason someone would be driving down this road was if they intended to come to this prison or they got lost.

Even knowing this and that it was highly unlikely that someone was just riding down here to try and rape and murder everyone here, Kallen had learned the hard way in life that you prepare for the worst so she kept herself hidden and waited to see who this was and why they were here. Kallen peeked over the hood again and could now see the vehicle coming down the road. It was some sort of truck or jeep but Kallen couldn't see it clearly enough yet to identify it. She kept her eyes on it as it got closer and finally, she was able to see that it was one of those military hummer things.

"Why the hell would the military be coming out here," Kallen asked herself out loud? This was a federal prison and all she thought, but if they were gonna send out military to evacuate the prison then they'd have done that a week ago when they had stopped feeding the women here. Kallen kept watching as the vehicle got closer and couldn't see any military insignia, but she could see one of those big antennae on the back and figured that the government probably had unmarked military vehicles just like cops had unmarked cars. Still, even under normal circumstances Kallen had little trust for anyone and this was so far removed from normal that she had no intention of just running out and flagging down a vehicle even if it did look like a military truck.

The hummer turned off the main road and onto the road leading to the secondary employee entrance gate. It didn't slow down and just kept barreling towards the gate and then through it. Kallen thought that whoever was in the hummer was lucky this was the rear employee gate to a minimum-security prison instead of one of the maximum-security joints around the state. The gate hadn't slowed the hummer at all and had seemed like something put there just for show in its wake.

The hummer was headed towards Kallen so she scuttled around the car she was hiding behind to position the car between her and the approaching vehicle. The driver of the hummer slammed on its brakes when it was in front of the ambulance and squealed to a halt. The driver's door flew open and a girl no older than the one who had attacked Kallen earlier jumped out of the hummer and ran to the back doors. She jerked the doors open and jumped into the back of the ambulance. After a few seconds Kallen heard the girl start chanting "fuck" over and over again.

The girl jumped back out of the ambulance and looked around frantically still chanting her one-word mantra. Kallen saw fear and desperation and anger in the girl's eyes and recognized that look far more than she cared to think about. That look had such a disarming effect on Kallen that she had stepped out from behind the car without even realizing she had and the word "Hey", fell out of her mouth. The girl whirled on her toes and that was when Kallen saw the gun in the girl's hand as it came up and fired a thankfully wild and wide shot to the left of her head. Kallen ducked instinctively and then said, "I'm unarmed! Don't shoot!"

The girl waved the gun towards the car Kallen was hunkered behind and said in a trembling voice, "Are you bitten?"

"What," Kallen questioned back?

"Are you fucking bitten," the girl yelled back in an obviously angrier tone.

"I don't understand what you mean," Kallen replied. "Bitten by what?"

"By one of them goddamnit," the girl yelled. "What the fuck do you mean you don't understand? Have you been living under a rock for the last 3 weeks?"

Kallen shook her head trying to figure out what the girl was talking about and then the girl who had attacked her after she'd gotten out of the prison came into her mind. The way the girl had been trying to bite at her came fully into her mind and then it clicked.

"No," Kallen yelled back. "I haven't been bitten. I was trapped in here when everything happened and I have no idea what's happening."

"Fuck," the girl said and lowered the gun. "I need help. My dad's been shot."

Kallen tentatively came out from behind the car and raised her hands to show her palms to the girl to show she was unarmed. The girl looked up at Kallen and the look in her eyes said she was defeated. Tears started from the girl's eyes and the gun slid out of her hand onto the ground at her feet.

Part 3: The Escape

1.

It was 3 in the morning when I was awakened by my dad quickly pulling clothes out of my dresser and hastily shoving them into my hiking pack.

"Dad," I said. "What's going on?"

My dad turned sharply to look at me. "Something terrible honey," he answered. "We've got to go as quick as we can. Throw some clothes on please."

"It's 3 in the morning Dad," I said looking at the digital clock beside my bed.

"I know baby," he said softly. "You can go back to sleep in the car."

By the time I reached the car sleeping was the furthest thing from my mind.

2.

The television was on when I came into the living room after throwing on some clothes. There was a *Breaking News* banner running across the bottom of the screen and below that were the words *Multiple Attacks Reported Across the Country*. Dad had the tv muted so I couldn't hear what the reporter was saying but I could see he was reporting live from somewhere. I grabbed the remote and unmuted the tv so I could hear what the reporter was talking about.

"I repeat," the reporter said, "If you live anywhere near the downtown area stay in your home. The police are doing their best to get..."

At that moment, a cop tackled the reporter and the camera followed the two to the ground. The cop was screaming and growling and hitting the reporter over and over, and then the cop bit the reporter on the cheek and ripped part of his face off. The tv immediately cut the live feed and went back to an obviously terrified young woman in the studio who was covering her mouth to stifle screams and had tears pouring down her eyes. After a few seconds she started saying "Oh God" repeatedly and they cut to a commercial.

I'm not sure when my dad had entered the room, but he saw me crying and staring at the tv in horror. He knelt on one knee in front of me and grabbed my shoulders.

"I'm sorry you saw that baby and I know you're scared, but we have to go **right now**," he said firmly.

I nodded dumbly at him and he stood back up and grabbed our hiking packs.

"I'm going to take these out to the car and make sure it's safe first. You stay right here, and I'll be back in a flash," my dad said.

"Dad, no," I cried.

"I'll be right back baby," he said. "I promise."

He opened the door and looked around in front of the house for just a second before running down the steps to the car and throwing the packs in the trunk. He ran back up the stairs to me waiting at the door.

"One last thing and then we're out of here," he said.

He went to the hall closet that had two separate deadbolt locks on it and quickly unlocked both locks and opened the door. Inside were several long riffles, a large black case, 4 handguns, and several ammo boxes. He pulled a shoulder holster off a hook on the inside of the door and put it on having to adjust the straps slightly for the weight he'd put on in the last few years since mom had died and then grabbed one of the handguns. He checked the magazine to make sure it had ammo in it, slid the magazine back into the weapon and chambered a round. He did this again with an identical handgun then checked the other two handguns also and slid one into the back of his pants and the other back into the belt holster it had been in and attached that to his belt.

He pulled his old marine duffel bag off the one shelf in the closet and filled it with the remaining guns and ammo. He threw the bag over his shoulder, it had to weigh a ton, and then grabbed the large black case in his other hand. He didn't bother locking the closet back and headed straight for the front door where I was standing.

"Alright sweety," he said as gently as possible. "We're going to be just fine, but I need you to do exactly as I say at all times, okay?"

I nodded dumbly again, and he reached up and wiped the tears from my cheeks.

"Let's do this," he said as he grabbed my hand with his free hand and opened the front door.

We ran down the stairs to the car and went to the passenger side. I opened the door and got in and he opened the back door and threw the duffle and black case into the back. As he was getting into the car our neighbor Mrs. Patterson stepped onto her front stoop and yelled to him.

"Tommy," she yelled! "What's going on? The news said there have been attacks and it looked like a policeman killed a reporter on live tv."

"Go back inside Janey," my dad yelled back. "It isn't safe."

As if to prove my dad's point our other neighbor, Mr. Andrews, came running from his house across the street straight at Mrs. Patterson. He launched himself at her sending them both flying through her screen door. I could hear her screams and Dad hesitated to get in the car for just a minute and then got in and slammed the key in the ignition.

"Dad we have to help her," I cried.

"There's nothing we can do honey," he replied with tears in his eyes. "We have to go."

I still think about Mrs. Patterson a lot, and I know Dad was right, but I can't help but feel guilty that we couldn't save her. She didn't deserve to die like that.

3.

Mom had been the one who said we had to live in the city. She said the schools were better and she liked being able to go shopping right down the street. Dad had agreed because he always tried his best to make her happy, but he would have been happier in a cabin out in the woods growing his own food and hunting. Now, mom's choice of living in the city, was turning out to be a nightmare.

Dad tried to take side roads and avoid the main streets, but even so the traffic was still bad. It could have been worse though if Dad hadn't had insomnia and been up writing with the news on for background noise. By 6 am the traffic was at a complete standstill and much of the city was on fire and in complete chaos. But by that time, we had made it out of the city and were headed north and only knew just how bad it had gotten from the news still being reported on the radio.

Before we could get out of the city, as Dad turned onto the road leading to the highway, we almost hit the cars that had wrecked into each other in front of us. The drivers of the cars were standing in the road yelling at each other.

"Are you fucking retarded," one man screamed at the other?!

"Me," the other man questioned back just as loudly?! "You ran into me asshole!"

"You were stopped in the middle of the road moron," the first man yelled back balling his fists at his sides. "What kind of dipshit just stops in the middle of the fucking road?"

"Some lady ran in front of my goddamn car asshole," the second man responded. "Was I just supposed to run her ass over?!"

Dad turned to me and said, "Stay here and lock the doors."

"Dad don't," I pleaded. "Let's just turn around and go the other way to the highway."

"It'll take too long honey," he said. "I just need to get the guys out of the way."

He opened the door and started walking towards the men. When he was about 10 feet away a woman, the woman the second man almost hit presumably, came running and screaming out of the alley to the right. The two men didn't notice her at all, but Dad saw her and pulled one of his guns from the shoulder holster.

"Stop ma'am," Dad yelled at the woman.

She either didn't hear him or just didn't care because she kept running towards the two arguing men.

"Stop ma'am," Dad yelled again and raised the gun to aim at her.

She was 3 feet from the men when they finally noticed her running at them and both turned towards her surprised and confused.

"Stop goddamnit," Dad yelled again, and again she kept going.

I could just hear Dad say, "Fuck," under his breath and then he shot her in the leg.

The bullet hit just below the kneecap and the lower half of that leg seemingly exploded into a cloud of blood and bone fragments. She fell to the ground a foot from the man who had almost hit her with his car. Despite having just been shot in the leg, the woman frantically reached out with both hands and seized the man in front of her by the leg. The man was easily twice her size, but she jerked him off his feet like he was a ragdoll and crawled up his body with such speed that he never had any chance of fighting her off. She slammed her face into his in what resembled the most violent and unwanted kiss in all of history, and then jerked her head back in one swift motion taking the man's lips with her. Dad shot a second time and the top half of the woman's head exploded spraying blood and brains onto the man below her who now had no lips.

"What the fuck," the other man who had been arguing screamed! "I'm fucking out of here man!"

The man ran back to his car and threw it in reverse to get around the car he'd run into in front of him. He hit the gas and lurched backwards running over the remaining leg of the woman and then the head of the man who he had been arguing with. If I live to be 100 years old, I will never forget the sound of that man's head exploding under the weight of the car. I felt myself about to be sick and threw my door open to vomit in the street rather than on myself or in the car. The man threw the car into drive and slammed on the gas leaving a trail of burnt rubber, blood, and brains on the road as he sped off.

After I threw up twice, I yelled, "Dad!"

My dad was already running back to the car and he yelled, "Shut the door and lock it now!"

I did as he asked and a few seconds later he was back in the car with me and he locked all the doors. He sat there for a minute just staring out the windshield at the two mangled bodies in the street in front of us.

"Fuck," he said. "FUUUUUCK!"

He was crying, but I don't think he noticed at all. He hit the steering wheel and cursed again. I reached out and grabbed his arm.

"We have to go," I said. "There might be more people like that lady out here."

As if on que someone started screaming nearby and that seemed to snap my dad back into action.

"Get your shit together marine," Dad mumbled to himself. "Right. We gotta go."

He buckled himself in, put the car in drive, and maneuvered the car around the bodies in the street so as not to defile them any more than they had already endured. As we drove out of the city, we heard a several explosions behind us, but neither of us turned to see what had happened. To quote Shakespeare, "That way madness lies."

4.

Mom had pestered Dad for years to trade in his Hummer for something more fuel efficient and practical for city living. Dad had held firm on that one though and had said that if things ever went bad and we had to get somewhere safe that she'd be glad he kept the Hummer. She wasn't here to be glad he'd kept it, but I was, and looking back on it now that things have calmed down, I think that Hummer is one of the biggest reasons we made it out alive.

We drove up on an ambulance on the way out of the city that had crashed into a streetlamp and Dad slowed down as we came close not knowing what had happened or if anyone was hurt. Just as Dad was about to stop to help, one of the EMTs stumbled around from the back of the ambulance. One of his eyes was hanging from its socket and his left arm was missing. He seemed completely dazed and unaware of where he was or what had happened to him. We had been so focused on the EMT that we didn't see the other man who had come around the front of the ambulance. The other man screamed in a deep guttural unhuman voice like that of some dangerous animal. The injured EMT came out of his daze some when he heard the sound and noticed us in front of him.

"Help," the EMT tried to call out and ended up spitting up blood.

The man who had come around from the front of the ambulance immediately turned towards the EMT and sprinted full speed at him. Before Dad could even think about trying to help the EMT, the sprinting man had tackled him to the ground and started slamming his head into the ground so hard that the back of the EMT's head nearly exploded.

I screamed out and Dad slammed his foot on the gas speeding away as fast as he could.

"It's going to be okay baby," Dad said. "We're going to get out of here and get somewhere safe."

I couldn't stop crying and I was shaking all over. It was like I was trapped in a nightmare. This couldn't really be happening. I closed my eyes as tightly as possible and as impossible as I thought it would be, I drifted off into sleep.

5.

"Wake up Aisling," Dad said.

I jerked awake instantly and yelled, "Zombies!"

Dad jerked a bit behind the wheel then said, "It's okay sweety. We're safe. Those weren't zombies honey. They were just sick or on some drug or something."

"Sick," I questioned more curtly than I meant to. "They were eating people Dad. What disease or drug makes you want to eat people?"

"Remember when that guy got high on bath salts and bit that other man's face off," Dad replied?

"You think someone put bath salts in the water or something," I asked?

"I don't know," he answered. "But I do know that zombies aren't real so there has to be a rational explanation for what's happening."

I let that settle in my mind for a bit and decided he had to be right.

"Where are we," I asked finally looking around?

We were driving down a dirt road through what looked like a forest but none of the trees looked like the ones she was used to seeing in the state parks around Tennessee where they lived that dad loved to take her hiking and camping.

"State Park in Illinois," he said.

"Why aren't we on the highway anymore," I asked tentatively.

Dad didn't answer right away and looked over at me for a minute. "There was a wreck," he said and paused for a second. "A couple of them actually. People are scared and not paying attention on the roads." He paused again and then said, "I think some of them were sick too. You didn't need to see any more of that."

"Why did you wake me up then," I asked?

"There's a military Hummer behind us," he said. "It's been following us since we turned off the main road into the state park."

I jerked my head around to look and then said, "Why aren't we stopping? Can't they help us?"

Dad didn't answer and I thought he might not have heard me.

"Dad," I questioned? "Why don't we stop and ask them for help?"

He looked over at me for a second and finally said, "If they wanted to help, they would have stopped us when they saw us, not follow us into this state park."

He looked at me again and I could see worry in his eyes.

"Whatever is going on," he began, "it isn't like anything that's ever happened before. That's a marine vehicle which should not be deployed on U.S. soil unless the president has issued a state of emergency and martial law. All the radio stations have gone silent and the cell signals died about 2 hours ago so I can't check the internet to see what the official statement is as to what is being done to handle the situation. If martial law has been put in effect, then we're breaking about 12 federal laws right now. I have no idea what orders these men have been given," he paused again, "but if it's as bad as I think it is then they may have orders to contain whatever this is by whatever means necessary."

"But we aren't sick Dad," I said. "They wouldn't arrest us if we aren't sick, would they?"

He looked over at me gravely and said, "I'm worried they won't arrest us at all or care that we aren't sick."

We drove on in silence deeper into the forest for several more miles when suddenly we heard a squelch from a speaker and then a loud voice said, "Pull the vehicle over."

Dad did not stop.

"Pull the vehicle over now," the voice said again.

Dad slowed down and as he did, he pulled one of his guns from its holster and placed it under his leg.

"Dad," I started nervously.

"Quiet honey," he interrupted. "Let me handle this."

He brought the Hummer to a stop on the side of the dirt road and the other Hummer pulled in behind us. Dad unbuckled his seatbelt and waited for the marines to get out of their Hummer. Two marines got out of the Hummer and immediately aimed their riffles at our car as they approached.

"Step out of the vehicle with your hands up," the driver yelled.

"Get in the floor baby," Dad whispered at me.

I unbuckled and curled myself into the floor in front of my seat.

Dad opened his door and stepped out of the car leaving the gun he'd removed from its holster in his seat and leaving the door open.

He raised his hands over his head and said, "What seems to be the problem guys?"

"Do you have any weapons on you sir," the driver asked?

"Weapons," Dad questioned back? "Why would I have weapons? I'm just headed out to do some camping."

The driver didn't say anything and shot Dad in the chest. He flew back into the door and slid down it.

"Dad," I screamed!

"There's another one in the car," the driver yelled! "Deal with her private!"

The other marine moved quickly over to my door and as he was opening it another shot rang out.

"What the fu," the other marine began to say and then the window exploded out and half of the marine's face disappeared in a spray of blood and bone and he fell beside the car.

My ears were ringing and I had no idea what had just happened. I looked over to where Dad was, and he was on his knees with the gun in one hand and the other holding his chest.

"Dad," I yelled and scrambled up out of the floor and across the seat to him.

"Jesus," Dad said. "That shit hurts every time."

He pulled his jacket open and revealed his flak jacket underneath.

"That's twice this thing has saved my ass kid," he said and smiled at me.

I threw my arms around him and he grunted and winced as I hugged him tighter than I'd ever hugged him before.

He hugged me back tightly and said, "I'm okay baby. A little bruised I'm sure, but otherwise I'm fit as a fiddle."

I started bawling and through the tears I said, "I thought they killed you Dad. Why did he shoot you? You didn't do anything!"

"They had orders I'm sure," he said. "Contain by any means necessary. Which means we can't trust any military we run into. We stick to back roads and we don't stop for anyone else again."

He stood up and said, "Don't move. I'll be back in just a minute."

He walked over to the driver who was not moving pointing the gun at him and put one foot on the man's riffle then reached down to check for a pulse. He stood back straight and removed his foot from the riffle. Then he walked around the car and found the other marine gulping for air through a mouth and throat that was half missing and full of blood.

Dad put a foot on the man's riffle and bent down close to him. "I'm sorry, but you followed the wrong car today marine."

Dad put his gun under what was left of the man's chin and pulled the trigger.

6.

We didn't run into anyone else for a long time as we continued through the forest and we didn't speak for the next hour.

I finally broke the silence asking Dad, "Where are we going?"

Dad didn't answer right away and when I looked over at him, I could see sadness in his eyes. After a minute he said, "When mom died, I found out she had taken out a large insurance policy on all of us. I used some of it to buy a cabin and stock it with supplies just in case something ever went terribly wrong and we needed a safe place to go.

Before today I questioned if I was crazy for doing it and last year, I almost sold the place. Now I'm really glad I didn't."

"A cabin," I crowed. "Why haven't we been there before now?"

He laughed a bit and said, "Because you hate the cold Ash."

"Cold," I said curiously? "Where is it?"

He looked over and smiled then said, "Alaska."

"Alaska," I exclaimed! "We're driving to Alaska!"

He laughed again and answered, "Jesus, I hope not! We're headed to a friend's house in Illinois. He's a close friend from the corps, a brother really, and he owns a helicopter. I called him before the phones went dark and he said he'll be waiting on us. Hopefully, he's still there and we can take the chopper up to the cabin."

"I have always wanted to visit Alaska," I said. "But I always thought it would be a vacation or something instead of running from the zombie apocalypse."

Dad turned towards me to say something and I cut him off saying, "I know. I know. There's no such thing as zombies. But this is pretty close, so I think it still counts as a zombie apocalypse."

He laughed at that and we continued through the forest.

I turned on the radio and scanned through the full FM band but only found static. I switched over to AM and scanned again, but still got nothing. I tried my phone and as Dad had said I got no signal.

Not thinking I said, "Damnit all to hell," and then immediately slapped a hand across my mouth and said through my hand, "Sorry Dad."

Dad laughed and said, "No. Damnit all to hell is pretty spot on Ash. Look in the back seat and grab that CB radio I pulled out the marine's Hummer."

I reached back into the seat and grabbed the radio. I'd seen these in movies before and said, "Isn't this what truckers use to talk to each other?"

"Not just truckers honey," he answered. "Cops, the military, and even just regular citizens use them all the time. They even can pick up ham radio signals if they're close enough."

"You can't make a radio out of ham Dad. That's just silly," I scoffed at him.

He giggled at that and said, "Ham is just the term used for amateur radio enthusiasts. They sell all the things you need to build your own personal radio broadcasting system at electronics stores and online. Those don't use radio towers to boost their signal, so they have a short range of only a few miles unless they have used an antenna to boost the broadcast. It's still more likely that we'll find someone on these short bands than any of the FCC regulated large stations."

I plugged the radio into the cigarette lighter hole and turned it on. As soon as it was powered on a voice came through the small front speaker and we heard just how bad it was.

7.

After 10 minutes of listening somberly I turned the radio off, and Dad didn't protest. What we'd heard in that 10 minutes was the most horrific thing I've ever heard. The voice on the radio was General Haden, and he was passing along the official statements and orders handed down by the moron in the oval office. The orders were direct, absolutely horrible, and violated multiple constitutional and international laws. The official statement was that a biological weapon in the form of weaponized rabies had been used by terrorists to infect the citizens of several countries worldwide. So far as they knew no one had been able to contain the outbreak with any measure of success and it had spread faster than anything anyone had ever seen. Infection spread through bodily fluids and given the nature of how rabies effects both people and animals alike, the infected were prone to biting and were transferring the virus at an uncontrollable rate. Symptoms showed within one to two hours of infection and common rabies treatments had proved useless. The short of it all was that, if you got bit by one of the infected it was game over.

The orders the general had been given and passed down the ranks were to assume anyone they encountered may already be infected and to approach with extreme caution, which was good. What wasn't so good is that they had orders to assume that anyone trying leave an outbreak area was infected and should be treated as such. After the orders were given another voice came on the radio and asked if he had heard the orders correctly. The general confirmed that he had, and the voice came back saying, "We can't just gun down American citizens sir!"

The general replied, "You have your orders. These orders have been standing for the last 6 hours and any act to disobey or disregard these orders will be considered an act of sedition. Given the current state of martial law anyone engaged in an act of sedition will be shot on sight. Is that clear sergeant?"

"Yes sir," the voice replied before I had shut off the radio.

We drove on in silence for a while longer, then I finally said, "What are we going to do now Dad? The military is gonna be everywhere."

"The plan hasn't changed Ash," Dad answered. "The only thing that's changed is that we now have two groups of highly dangerous and unstable people to try and avoid."

8.

We drove for another several hours and it got dark again. Dad didn't want to risk driving with the lights on and being noticed so he pulled over off of the road and into the woods slowly as to not wreck and ruin our only means of transportation. He said we'd try to get some rest in the hummer and hopefully be up to his friend's cabin before noon tomorrow.

I climbed into the back seats and laid down knowing for sure I wouldn't sleep; knowing that as soon as I closed my eyes all the horrors of the last 48 hours would fill my mind. But they didn't. I closed my eyes and there was only darkness and then I was out cold until the brightness of sunlight finally woke me up.

Dad was driving again already and I was surprised I hadn't woken up when we started moving. I must have been more exhausted than I'd realized. I let out a thoroughly overexaggerated yawn so Dad would know I was awake and he laughed at this and then said, "You think I didn't hear you moving around back there so you thought you'd let out a yeti cry?"

I giggled at this and leaned forward from the back seat to kiss him on the cheek.

"Are we close Dad," I asked?

"About 15 miles out," he answered. "But I'm not sure how long that's going to take."

Before I could ask why I looked forward out of the window and answered the question rising in my mind before it could reach my lips. We weren't on the road any more.

I timidly asked, "Do I even want to know why we're driving through the woods?"

"There were 6 separate military convoys that came far closer to us last night than I liked at all," Dad answered. He continued, "I'm afraid this whole thing has gone really bad honey. We have to avoid other people like the plague, and that includes the military and the cops. **Especially** the military and the cops."

After a few seconds he chortled sourly and said, "No pun intended."

At first, I didn't get what he meant and then thought: *avoid other people like the plague*. Other people were the plague now. Maybe they had been all along. Whatever was happening it was almost surely something that other people had done that had caused it.

As if reading my mind Dad said, "This isn't natural!"

He quickly realized how absurd that simple statement was and continued saying, "I mean, like not something that just came from nature. This isn't like some crazy virus that just thawed out of the permafrost because of climate change or some shit. Somebody **made** this. Somebody fucking **did** this."

I didn't say anything. What could I say? He was thinking the same thing I was. Maybe some Charles Campion style screw up like in Stephen King's *The Stand* perhaps? A spilled vial and a door that didn't close in time? Maybe it was terrorists. They'd gotten more and more industrious over the years and it wasn't outside the realm of possibility they'd cook up some bioweapon they didn't fully understand and end up killing us all.

No matter where or who had done this, the term *human error* kept flashing like an electric sign in my mind.

I said those words aloud softly, "Human error."

Dad stopped the hummer, put it in park, and looked out the front windshield. He stared out there for a moment and then said softly, "Human fucking error."

I put my hand on my dad's shoulder and said softly, "It doesn't matter."

He turned his head and looked back at me. Our eyes met and I wished that my hopelessness wasn't clear in my eyes but I could see by the sorrow rising on his face that I was failing to hide my feelings.

"I just mean," I said, "it doesn't matter how it started right now because the only thing that matters is getting somewhere safe... right?"

Dad smiled as best he could and said, "Yeah baby. You're right. Let's get out of here."

He reached out and grabbed the back of my head lightly bringing my forehead to his lips and planting a kiss there then turned back around and began driving again.

After another 30 minutes or so Dad came to the actual road again and stopped. He sat there for several minutes and slowly scanned the road. He was clearly also listening for other vehicles and I did my best to be as quiet as possible. Finally, he put his hand on the gear shift and said, "Fuck it," and then drove out onto the road.

"We need to make up time and honestly I'm pretty sure those troops should have moved on by now into the nearby cities," Dad said. "We'll get out of this park and these woods and try to make our way up taking the back roads as much as possible. We've got two 10-gallon tanks of gas on the back of the Hummer I swiped off the Marines that we ran into but we don't have a map so we need to stop at a gas station if we can find one that seems safe."

Remembering something I had seen on some YouTube video I pulled out my cellphone and pulled up my gps. I leaned up from behind Dad and held my phone out where he could see it and said, "No map needed Dad. Gps works without a cell signal or service."

"What," Dad said surprised?

"Yep," I retorted. "As long as the satellites are up there in space and in proper orbit then we can find our way."

"Where did you learn that little gem," he asked?

"YouTube or TikTok," I answered. "Not sure which."

"You know what this means right," he asked?

"What," I asked in return?

"It means you just got promoted to navigator," he answered with a laugh. "Now climb up here with me and tell me where we're going."

I climbed up into the passenger seat and said, "Do you want to try to at least get to a highway or just stay all back-roads?"

He didn't answer right away and after a few minutes he said, "You remember how hard it was to get out when we left?"

It was a rhetorical question and I waited for him to continue.

"We only barely did get out," he continued. "So, it would follow that the same thing would be the case most everywhere. That means that realistically the highways and interstates, aside from the onramps and offramps, should be fairly passable."

"That makes sense," I said. "But what about the army?"

"That is a whole other can of worms," he answered. "Their orders are to contain this by any means, but given what we saw when we got out that mission has been called a failure so that means they will very likely move to a more *aggressive* strategy."

"That doesn't sound good," I said. "What's more *aggressive* than shoot anybody you see?"

He didn't answer.

"What," I asked again, "they gonna nuke us all?"

"Probably not," he said flatly. "That would be overkill. You have to be able to rebuild. What they **would do** is pull out all troops that have not yet come in contact with the infected, leave the ones who had regardless of their infection or lack thereof, and then send in strategic air-strikes."

He looked over at me for just a moment. I could see that he was being completely honest and he could see that this scared the hell out of me.

"Theorizing isn't the right answer here," he said reaching out and turning on the CB radio.

9.

The *information*, if you could call it that, we'd learned from listening in on the CB radio again had been jumbled and confusing but what was clear was that the chain of command was crumbling if not already fully broken. Orders had been given to send in bombers just like Dad had thought but only 2 squadrons actually followed those orders leveling most of Arizona and Florida. A nuclear power plant outside Dallas Texas had gone critical with no one to keep it in check and following a massive explosion was now leaking large scale radioactive contamination into the entirety of Texas, Nevada, Arizona, and down into Mexico. That area of the planet might be uninhabitable for the next 50 years with how much radiation was just spewing out. Of course, habitability was the least of the world's problems right now since this virus had spread to the entire planet and people were getting infected so fast that it was hard to believe anyone was going to live through this to inhabit anything. As for their neck of the woods and what troubles they were going to have to face, that was actually harder to grasp. From what communications were coming through Ash could only piece together at least half the troops in the area had gone AWOL and just abandoned whatever posts they'd been assigned to man. What troops hadn't deserted were now running around killing anyone and everyone they saw without question. At one point a man came on the radio and asked for help at check-point delta saying that at least two officers were sick and then screams issued from the radio and it abruptly went silent.

Dad reached out and shut the radio off and neither of us said anything for a while. Everything was falling apart and it had only been 3 days... or had it been 4? I couldn't remember at this point and it didn't even really matter. I couldn't help but feel like things had become absolutely hopeless at this point.

After a few minutes Dad pulled out his phone and fidgeted with it for a minute and then said, "We need something less grim for a bit."

After a second the Sevendust song Black started playing. Dad let it play for a bit and then looked over at me and started singing along with the chorus, "I'm minding my own business. I ain't doing nothing wrong. I ain't doing nothing wrong!"

I joined in with him and we started driving again.

"I'm minding my own business! I ain't doing nothing wrong! I ain't doing nothing wrooooong!"

10.

It took us another 20 minutes to finally reach Dad's friend's cabin and we jammed out to Sevendust and Nonpoint the whole way and I loved Dad for letting us escape into the music for a while. Not to mention that these bands were something that Dad and I had shared that had been all ours. Mom had never been a fan of me listening to such 'adult themes', but Dad had always said that the real world was hard and that we have to be strong and able to fight and the only way to do that is to know what you're up against. Dad said these bands, and many of the others we listened to together, told stories of real hardship and the struggle to overcome.

By the time we got out of the Hummer at the cabin we were both in much better spirits and feeling pretty hyped up. That feeling lasted all of 2 minutes as we walked up to the door of the cabin and saw the bullet holes in the door and walls and the windows shot out.

"Fuuuuuuck," Dad exclaimed. "This does not look good."

He had pulled one of his guns the moment we'd gotten out of the Hummer and now he pulled the other and looked at me.

"Ash," he started, "you know I can't stand the idea that you would ever have to use a gun on another human being. You know I swore to never take another innocent life after I left the Marines, and that I would never want you to experience the heartbreak of taking a life." He paused and looked sorrowfully at me with tears building in his eyes, "But we can't afford the luxury of morality if we want to make it through this. I've already had to break my promise not to kill, and now I have to ask you to be stronger than you've ever been in your life."

He handed me the other gun and said, "You remember what I taught you?"

"Yes Dad," I said with tears welling in my eyes.

"Repeat the lessons back please," he asked.

"Aim center mass," I started choking back tears. "Legs slightly spread and one leg slightly back to help brace for the kick. Deep breath. Squeeze, don't pull, the trigger."

"Good girl Ash," Dad responded and put a hand on my shoulder. "You've got this. We're gonna make it out."

11.

The cabin was absolutely wrecked. Bullets had torn through everything in the place and there was glass and debris covering everything. Soldiers had emptied entire magazines into this cabin indiscriminately to try to kill anyone or anything in it, but it looked as though they hadn't come in to make sure the place was clear afterwards which seemed sloppy and very unlike the military Dad had described. Why would they just shoot up a place not even knowing if there was anyone in it and then not even check to see if anyone had been in there? Were they afraid of getting infected somehow?

As if reading my mind Dad said, "This is wrong. Why didn't they clear this place after unloading on it like that?"

We continued into the cabin and made our way through the living room and into the narrow hall that led to three doors. The first door to the left as we came into the hall was open and revealed a bathroom which had also been wrecked by bullets and was now leaking water from at least 3 different places. The next two doors, one at the very end of the hallway and one to the right, were both closed. Dad motioned at the door in the back for me to open it so he could clear whatever room was behind the door. We had done this before when playing paintball with some of dad's friends and their kids and I remembered just how to do it; body positioned at the wall by the hinges so when the door opens Dad has a clear shot on anything that may be inside. I opened the door fast just like he'd shown me and made sure to stay clear of the opening. Just a closet with towels and toiletries that were also riddled with bullets.

Dad gestured to the last door and I repeated the whole operation. This door opened onto a bedroom which was also destroyed by gunfire but this room also had blood splattered across it in several places. Dad gestured for me to hold in the hall while he entered the room cautiously. "Terry," Dad questioned lightly? I watched from the hallway as my dad walked around the bed to the far side of the room and then froze. "Holy fuck," he said and threw his hand over his mouth as a retching sound came up in his throat.

He looked back at me and threw a hand up at me, "Stop," he said quickly. "Don't come in here. An infected got in here and got Terry and then got gunned down when the soldiers came through. You don't want to see this."

He was right. I didn't want to see it. I hadn't wanted to see any of it. I didn't want any of this to be happening at all and it was all I could do to keep from bursting out in tears but right now was not the time for that. I had to keep it together so I could help my dad get us out of here. I composed myself and then said, "What now? I didn't see a helicopter out there anywhere and even if we did find it who would fly it?"

"I'm not sure honey," he answered back. "Let's get out of this cabin and let me think for a minute."

I waited at the door for dad and then we made our way back out of the cabin and walked back over to the Hummer. Dad holstered his gun and I handed the other gun back to him.

"You still need a gun Ash. Gimme a sec," he said and walked around the Hummer to the back and grabbed a small handgun from one of the bags in the back. "This one will be better for you. It's got a lot less kick to it."

He handed me the gun and a thigh strap holster to keep it in. I strapped the holster onto my right thigh and secured the gun in it. With that done dad started pacing in front of the Hummer trying to figure out what our next move should be. After a few minutes he said, "Pull up the GPS. Let's see what's close by."

12.

After staring at the phone for several minutes dad said, "Okay. We've got two options. We can go here," he pointed at a dot on the phone's map labeled Greenville Airport then scrolled the map up and said, "or we can go here," and pointed to a new dot labeled FCI Greenville.

"What does FCI stand for," I asked him?

"Federal Corrections Institution," he answered. "It's a federal prison. If we can't find a helicopter at the airport then we might be able to grab a prison bus from the prison. Those busses are reinforced and almost surely bulletproof. If we end up having to drive then we'll want something with more protection than this Hummer can provide."

"Okay," I said tentatively, "but who's going to fly the helicopter if we do find one?"

"I will," dad answered. "I've flown a few times but never solo. It's not too difficult since I know the basics," he paused, "I just hope the landing goes smoother than the other times I tried to do it."

"Maybe we should just go for the bus," I said nervously.

"Maybe," he answered back, "but the chopper will be faster and we should at least see if it's an option. I've got a feeling that airport is going to be all emptied out."

He handed my phone back to me and said, "Let's get moving while we've still got some daylight."

13.

Dad said we could probably stop worrying about military after what we'd heard on the radio and decided we'd make our way back out onto the main roads and try to get into Greenville before nightfall. The roads leading out to the highway were littered with wrecked or abandoned cars and it took us a long time to get through it all and to the actual highway. As we pulled up to the turn onto the highway there was a huge pileup of cars in both lanes and even down into the ditches on either side of the road. Dad thought he could squeeze the hummer by on the right side driving through a weak chain-link fence and the field it was fencing off. As he drove through cautiously, I looked over at the cars to our left and saw that they were all riddled with bullet holes and most contained dead bodies.

"Oh god," I said quietly and saw my dad glance over in that direction and see the grim scene that I'd seen.

"I'm sorry," he said somberly, "but we're probably gonna see a lot more things like this," he paused for a moment and then finished with, "probably a lot worse things actually and we have to just take a breath and keep going."

"I know," I replied keeping the tears welling in my eyes at bay. "It's just... so much."

"I know honey," he soothed. "I know."

We drove through the field and made it onto the highway and it was almost completely empty except a few scattered vehicles full of bullet holes. We made good time with the roads so clear until we got closer into Greenville's actual city limits where we hit more wrecks and shot up vehicles. It took us another twenty minutes to navigate the wreckage and make it to the Greenville airport but before we even got there, we knew we probably weren't going to find a helicopter or a plane there because of the plume of smoke rising from the exact place we were heading. As we pulled up on the small rural airport my heart sank seeing the destruction. There were several wrecked cars in the parking lot, two still on fire, a plane that had either crashed or been blown up somehow, and every building at the airport was on fire.

Dad stopped the Hummer, put it in park, and just stared at the scene without saying anything. After a few seconds he drew in a deep breath and then sighed. He put the Hummer back in gear and said, "Off to the prison then," and started driving again.

We drove down the highway for several more miles and then came almost to the junction to get onto the highway that led to the prison but stopped at the gas station on the corner first. Dad pulled the

Hummer into the parking lot and said, "Wait here. The pumps are still on and hopefully they'll still work with a credit card."

He got out of the Hummer and swiped his card and then said, "Yes," and started punching in his pin on the keypad. A moment later he had lifted the pump out of its cradle and was filling the tank. He set the little notch that lets the pump autofill and walked back up to the driver's side window, "Figured I'd splurge and get the premium given the circumstances. Just need a couple gallons to get us-" he was saying and then a gunshot rang out and he stopped talking and stumbled forward.

"Dad," I screamed and started to climb out of the car. "No! Get down," he yelled back, and quickly ducked back to the back of the Hummer and jerked the nozzle out of the tank. He pulled out one of his guns and was holding his side with his other hand scanning for where the shot had come ran back up to the driver's door and jumped in quickly throwing the Hummer into reverse since he hadn't even actually shut it off and slammed his foot on the gas. Another shot came through the front windshield and right through the back, then dad raised his gun and shot through the front windshield twice and then slung the Hummer back onto the highway and into drive speeding away from the gas station and onto the highway that led to the prison.

I climbed back into my seat and said, "Did you get shot? What happened?"

He lifted the hand that had been holding his side and both the hand and his shirt where his hand had been were covered in blood and said, "Shit. That's not good," and then swerved a little before throwing his hand back over the wound wincing in pain at touching the gunshot.

"What am I supposed to do dad," I asked helplessly?

He stopped the Hummer, threw it in park, and said, "You're gonna have to drive. I need actual medical supplies. There will be stuff at the prison. I'm going to get in the back seat."

He climbed out of the Hummer and stumbled a bit as his feet didn't quite want to stay under him but he righted himself and got into the back after a second. I climbed over into the driver's seat, pulled the door shut, and moved the seat all the way up so I could actually reach the peddles. Tears were pouring down my face and my heart was beating so fast I thought it was going to explode. From the back seat dad said, "You can do this honey, but I need you to hurry okay?"

I wiped the tears away, threw the Hummer in gear, and said, "Okay. Just hold on. You're going to be okay," and then pushed my foot down on the accelerator.

14.

It took me ten minutes to get to the prison and when I saw the wreckage there it took everything I had not to just start screaming. The prison had been hit by a passenger plane, a 737 or some other big monster of a plane and I could see even from here that most of the place was rubble. What the hell sort of medical supplies would I be able to find in a pile of crushed concrete? Then I saw the ambulance in the parking lot and dared to hope again. "Hold on dad," I said. "Gotta drive through a gate."

I plowed through the gate with almost no resistance and barreled at the ambulance slamming on the brakes a few feet shy of it and threw the Hummer in park. I jumped out of the vehicle and ran to the ambulance throwing the back doors open and climbed inside. I had no idea what I was looking for. Gauze for sure. Alcohol to clean the shot. Tape to keep the gauze on.

I looked around franticly chanting "Fuck" over and over trying to figure this out and realizing that the ambulance had already been ransacked by someone and none of the things I needed were in the spots they should be in. I was losing it and I jumped back out of the ambulance still chanting "fuck" the whole time because I didn't know what else to say or do. My eyes darted around trying to find something, anything, that would help us in some way and then from behind me a woman's voice said, "Hey."

The gun dad had given me was out of its holster and in my hand before a realized it and I whirled around taking an immediate shot that, thankfully, missed the woman who had spoken. She ducked back behind the car she must have been behind when I pulled up and said, "I'm unarmed! Don't shoot!"

I waved the gun towards the car and tried not to sound like I was about to cry while I said, "Are you bitten?"

"What," the woman responded?

"Are you fucking bitten," I yelled back.

"I don't understand what you mean," the woman yelled back. "Bitten by what?"

"By one of them goddamnit," I yelled getting angrier by the second. How the hell could she not know what I meant by *are you bitten*? I didn't have time for this. "What the fuck do you mean you don't understand? Have you been living under a rock for the last 3 weeks," I added angrily?!

The woman didn't respond for a minute and I was about to start screaming at her when she finally said, "No. I haven't been bitten. I was trapped in here when everything happened and I have no idea what's happening."

"Fuck," I said absolutely defeated lowering the gun to my side. "I need help. My dad's been shot."

The woman stepped out from behind the car and held up her hands. She was wearing a prison guard uniform and the look in her eyes, the strength and determination there, was so opposite the despair I felt in that moment that I simply broke down and started crying dropping the gun at my feet.

The woman walked over to me, put a hand on my shoulder, and said, "Let me see if I can help. Is he in the truck?"

"In the back," I said as tears streaked down my cheeks.

The woman walked to the back of the Hummer and then turned back and said, "My name is Kallen," then turned back and opened the door. She leaned into the back some and said to dad, "Hey. My name is Kallen. Your daughter said you've been shot. I'm gonna try to help but I'm gonna need to move you onto the gurney in the back of that ambulance. Can you walk at all?"

I couldn't hear what dad said, but he must have answered because Kallen said, "Okay then big guy. You just lean on me all you need. One. Two. Three."

She lifted dad out of the back and onto his feet and when he stumbled, I thought she would drop him but she just dug in and steadied him and then helped him up into the ambulance. She got him laid onto the gurney and then grabbed a bag off the floor that had everything she needed to clean and fix a wound. She grabbed scissors out of the bag and cut dad's shirt down the middle so she could spread it open and see the gunshot. Kallen grabbed gauze and a brown bottle from the bag and then said to my dad, "I need you to let go of the wound now and let me see if I can patch you up, okay?"

Dad nodded and pulled his hand away and blood started leaking quickly out of the wound.

"Oh fuck," Kallen said and then her eyes shot over at me outside the ambulance as if to say 'I wish I hadn't said that out loud'.

"Is it bad," I asked her with far more hysteria in my voice than I liked hearing.

Kallen didn't answer immediately as she was running her hand around to my dad's back feeling for an exit wound and finally saying, "It isn't good. He's losing blood fast but it isn't too dark which is good. That means it missed his liver. If it had hit that he would have only had about five minutes. I can't find an exit wound which means the bullet is still in him. I can stitch him up and stop the external bleeding but I'm not a surgeon and even if I was, I don't have the tools here to remove a bullet or fix any internal damage." She looked at me for a moment and then said, "I can buy him time, but he needs an actual doctor and a lot more than I can do."

"Do whatever you can please," I said franticly.

She turned back and got to work cleaning the wound and then ripped open a bag of something with her teeth and said to my dad, "This is going to hurt a lot," and then pressed the contents of the bag into the gunshot. Dads back arched in agony and he tried to hold in a scream through clenched teeth. She pulled the bag away, poured more of the iodine on the wound and then wiped it with a gauze. "I'm gonna staple you up for now okay," she said to my dad and pulled a staple gun out of the bag. She squeezed the wound closed and put five staples into his skin to hold it closed. She cleaned it all one last time and then covered it with gauze and taped it up.

She put a hand on his shoulder and said, "Good job soldier. Rest for a minute and then we'll get you back in that truck and find a doctor."

Kallen jumped down out of the ambulance and then seemed to twitch a little. She reached in her pocket, pulled out a jar, dipped a finger in it, and then wiped that finger under her nose. She caught me watching her and said, "Menthol. I've got... sinus issues." The way she said it almost came off as a question but then she said, "What's your name?"

"Aisling," I answered.

"That's beautiful," she replied. "I've never heard that name before."

"It's Irish," I said. "My dad's family are Irish and he won a game of rock, paper, scissors, with my mom so he got to pick my name."

I was sure she would ask where my mom was but thankfully, she didn't. Instead, she said, "I don't know what happened out here but clearly things have gone very wrong around here. So, before we get going, while your dad takes a minute to catch his breath, why don't you tell me what's going on?"

I looked at the uniform again and then said, "You're not actually a guard, are you?"

"No ma'am I am not," Kallen answered immediately. "I had to take these clothes off of the poor dead woman in that car over there." She gestured to a car in a space a few spots away. "I was in that building when a plane flew into it and fell on the woman who had turned cannibal and who was trying to eat me."

My eyes must have bugged out further than I realized because Kallen laughed lightly at seeing the look on my face.

"We had all been trapped in there for the last," she paused and looked to be trying to figure something out then said, "6 or 8 days, I'm really not sure, without any guards coming through and no one serving meals so hunger was a bit of an issue."

"Did everyone else die when the plane hit the building," I asked?

"If they weren't already dead before then," Kallen answered.

"What," I asked?

"When the food stopped coming things got ugly," she answered. "Convicts aren't exactly known for having an abundance of patience or ethics."

"They just killed each other," I said horrified.

"Or killed themselves," Kallen said. "Go out on your own terms rather than starve to death."

"So, what about you," I asked?

"I had commissary foods," she answered back. "Enough for a week or two anyway and then I would have been in trouble too. Listen, I know that you've probably got a ton of questions for me and I'm also very much aware that telling you that I'm actually a convict doesn't exactly elicit a lot of reasons to trust me but I was very serious about your dad needing a doctor and I need to know what the hell is going on out here if I'm going to be able to help him."

It hit home with me right in that moment. He needed a doctor. Where there still doctors? Hospitals, like everything else, like this goddamn prison, were all either overrun or destroyed. Where the hell would we find a doctor?!

"Aisling," Kallen called? "What happened out here?"

"There aren't any doctors," I answered and started pacing back and forth in front of her.

"What," she asked back?

"There aren't any fucking doctors," I yelled! "No more doctors or hospitals or fucking surgeons, it's all gone! Everything is gone!"

Kallen reached out, grabbed me by the arms, and said, "Stop. I need you calm. **He** needs you calm. Tell me exactly what happened."

I looked at her and took a deep breath, "There's a virus. At first a couple people in a bunch of cities all over the world got sick with what the doctors said was SARS. After a few days in the hospital the people seemed like they were getting better and then a day later all hell broke loose. The sick people started attacking people and biting them or just beating people to death. The people who get bit get sick really quick and they attack anyone or anything around them. All the cities are either overrun or shot up by the military or worse. Me and my dad were trying to get up to our cabin in Alaska and try to ride the whole thing out but some piece of shit shot him when he was getting gas."

Kallen took her hands off my arms and began to chew on her right thumbnail while her left hand cradled her right elbow reminding me of that Rodin sculpture The Thinker. Her eyes darted around not really looking at anything but more rolling through ideas in her head. Finally, she said, "A hospital is still our best option. At the very least they'll have what I need to get the bullet out."

"I thought you said you couldn't remove the bullet," I asked her?

"No," Kallen answered. "I said I wasn't a surgeon and that even if I was, I didn't have the tools I needed here. Now help me move your dad back into your truck and please tell me you have a phone."

"It's a Hummer," I retorted smartly, "and the lines are all dead but yes I have a phone."

"I'm aware it's a Hummer sweety," Kallen retorted just as smartly, "but they're really all just cars and trucks, right? I mean, if the whole world just went to shit, we may as well dispense with the formalities as they say. Don't you think?" She smiled and it was one of the most honest and genuine smiles I had ever seen and then she continued, "And I was hoping for the phone to use GPS, but if you've got one, and if it's as bad as you say it is out there, then you've already been using it. Nearest hospital?"

She looked at me and that smile was there again. It was one of those smiles that touched deep in the eyes. Kallen's bluntness that bordered on rudeness was something I hadn't experienced before and I didn't know if I should be offended or just grateful for someone who seemed like they wouldn't bs me every step of the way. Since she was the only help for my dad it didn't matter; it was either trust her and accept this weird bluntness or let my dad die. I pulled out my phone and pulled up the map.

About the Author

Nicholas Stuart Bateman is a retired English tutor from northern Maine who now spends his days finishing the many stories he began writing in his youth. His style varies from satirically comedic to the deeply macabre.

This book was published and produced by Anti-Social Media. Anti-Social Media is a publication and production firm formed specifically to give a larger platform to independent content creators. We handle print, audio, and even film media offering editing, production, distribution, and marketing services. What makes us special is not the services we provide or even the exceptional quality of those services but rather the integrity and convictions of the company behind those services and our focus on the individual content creators.

Unlike traditional publishing and media distribution firms ASM values quality over quantity and values the rights of the content creators over the desire to get rich from their labor. We thoroughly vet each content creator who we sign with ASM and assure that they are someone whom we can stand behind as being representative of this company. We also assure that all content creators retain 100% of the rights to their work giving them the creative freedom to decide completely how and when their work is used.

If you enjoyed this book, please leave a review on Amazon and on Goodreads to help promote the work of this author. If you are an independent author or other independent content creator and would like to join the ASM team please email us at: antisocialmedia0@gmail.com

9 798215 720639